Mother, Sister, Daughter, Lover

Other books by Jan Clausen

- *After Touch* (Poetry; 1975)
- *Waking at the Bottom of the Dark* (Poetry; Long Haul Press, P.O. Box 592, Van Brunt Sta., Brooklyn, N.Y. 11215, distributed by The Crossing Press, 1979)
- Anthologies: *Cameos,* ed. Felice Newman (Crossing Press 1979)

Mother, Sister, Daughter, Lover

stories by Jan Clausen

THE CROSSING PRESS / Trumansburg, New York 14886

The Crossing Press Feminist Series

This book is for Anna Bulkin/remember the future

Acknowledgements

"Depending" first appeared in *Moving Out;* "The Warsaw Ghetto" in *Black Maria;* "Daddy" in *Women: A Journal of Liberation;* "Thesis: Antithesis" in *Heresies* No. 9. Parts I and II of "Today is the First Day of the Rest of Your Life" were published in *Frontiers,* and Part V in *Sinister Wisdom.* "Yellow Jackets" first appeared in *Calyx.*

The author wishes to thank Bernice Reagon for permission to use the book's title, which was inspired by her song "Every Woman"; and for the strength that is her music.

The Crossing Press Feminist Series

Front cover photograph—Marilyn Rivchin
Back cover photograph—Morgan Gwenwald
Cover and book design—Mary A. Scott

Printed in the U.S.A.

Library of Congress Cataloging in Publication Data

Clausen, Jan, 1950-
Mother, sister, daughter, lover.

(The Crossing Press feminist series)
1. Feminism--Fiction. I. Title.
PZ4.C6152Mo [PS3553.L348] 813'.54 80-16386
ISBN 0-89594-034-5
ISBN 0-89594-033-7 (pbk.)

CONTENTS

Depending

You gotta take the shit with the shineola.
—Old Brooklyn saying

Martha's kitchen. The wedge of afternoon light on the table as Martha pours tea. The luxury of cookies arranged for me on a plate. Her light, light kitchen, small but not cramped; cabinets painted blue; plants hanging in the high window; cats. Evidence of slow effort invested over years. Such comforts are beginning to assert a certain appeal, I recognize, thinking of my two dark, minimally furnished rooms on the other side of the park.

This afternoon Martha and I are talking about books, politics, the Tarot, cats, plants, food, problems of dependence and independence in relationships—but primarily we're talking about our incestuous circle of friends.

"Ellen is a cold bitch," I pronounce at last. This is the point I've been working myself up to for the past half hour.

Martha wrinkles her forehead at the daring of my assertion. "Could you be more specific?"

"Well, maybe I don't mean that," I say. "Maybe I just mean that I don't know how to handle feeling like I've been taken for a ride."

"Can't you accept the fact that you're angry at her?"

"I guess I've put in too much practice trying to understand her, trying to appreciate her reasons."

"I think you'd feel a lot better if you had it out with her."

"I'm sure you're right, but it's all very complicated and she's in fucking Minneapolis," I say, wearily tapping my cigarette.

"What's so complicated about it?" Martha queries in her irritating pseudo-therapeutic manner, sitting back and stroking the longhaired cat on her lap. Actually she's attempting to avoid taking risks, but she manages to look very impressive, very wise, sitting there in all that rich light, wearing a red linen wraparound top over her perfectly faded jeans, forty and stunningly beautiful in moments.

"It's complicated beyond belief. You and me and K.L. and Ellen–at best, it's a hopelessly tangled oedipal situation," I say. "Never mind triangles, this is at least a hexagon, or some bizarre cube in ten dimensions or something. Christ, whatever happened to simple friendship?"

"I don't know. The women's movement, maybe," Martha offers. "If all else fails, perhaps it would help to repeat, 'Ellen is a cold bitch,' ten or twenty times each morning upon rising."

"Thanks, buddy, I thought you were a friend of hers."

"What does that have to do with it?"

Severe guilt pangs surface, focusing my wandering attention on my motives. Why have I come to Martha to discuss Ellen, anyway? Is it some subtle attempt to sabotage their relationship?

"Perhaps we shouldn't talk about it."

"Just relax and stop berating yourself. You've been hurt. You're angry. Give yourself time and maybe things will change."

"Maybe I don't want anything to change. I'm too resentful." For Ellen lay with me, her long hair covering me like a trailing plant; she let me touch her everywhere, and when she started sleeping with K.L., she said, "Romance is dead."

"Were you in love with her?" Martha asks gravely, twisting her jade ring. The simplicity of forty!

"How should I know? I can't remember what 'in love' means. I just know I can't be her friend anymore."

Martha hums a few bars of the Supremes' song, "Mama Said, You Can't Hurry Love." "Well, maybe your environment is at fault. Maybe you need to meet a new crowd. Did you ever think of that?"

"I suppose I will eventually, when I get bored with my pain," I say petulantly.

"At least you and I are friends. That's something."

"Oh yes, but that's different." I don't say what I'm thinking: that it just makes things worse. She was Ellen's friend first. We're all prisoners in the house of incest.

All the same, I decide to go to the dance at Columbia. The radical middle-class vanguard is out in full force, stoned on beer, gyrating to the Stones or making out to the strains of Barry White in a crowded, smoke-filled arena. The costumes reflect our fantasies of who we are: lavender satin shirts leather belts keys boots crewcuts long skirts bow ties cowboy hats overalls earrings chains jeans jackets. All the faces look depressingly familiar.

Predictably, K.L. is here; she looks not a bit apologetic, asking me to dance. She has a new haircut, a sort of Jewish afro, and her shirt, unbuttoned halfway down to her wide, low-slung belt, opens just short of her nipples. It's a slow number, and we dance close, swaying in a parody of high school romance. I stumble every so often, never having learned how to dance properly. K.L. doesn't turn me on the least little bit.

"Did you have a nice time with Martha on Saturday?" she murmurs in my ear. She's leading; I'm letting her.

"It was all right. The play was wonderful." But how does she know Martha and I went out on Saturday?

"I've always thought you two should get to know each other better. She's a pretty farout lady, though I'm not very fond of those remote, genteel WASP airs she puts on sometimes."

K.L.'s authoritative stance irritates but also amuses me. Nobody else has such exquisite gall. Besides, I'm relieved to find we're talking normally, delighted to discover my hitherto unsuspected talent for pretending it doesn't matter about her and Ellen. Perhaps—stranger things have happened—there may even come a day when K.L. and I will be in a position to compare notes on that subject. Sometimes I catch myself at my calculations and feel like I'm trapped in a late Henry James novel. In my head, the future becomes a large chess board on which the infinite possible permutations and combinations of human relationships play themselves out. It's painful, but interesting.

"Actually, you and Martha have a lot in common," K.L. persists, an oily voice in my ear. She has the advantage of being about five inches taller than I am.

"What's this? Just what the fuck is all this?" I explode, really pissed off at last. "We went to a play. What's the big deal?"

"Relax," K.L. laughs down at me. "I'm joking. All the same, you're both romantics, you're both lonely and your signs are highly compatible."

"Romance is dead."

"Of course I realize she's practically old enough to be your mother."

"Ageism, ageism," I mutter, not quite as displeased as I sound. For it has never before occurred to me that Martha could be, as they say, *interested* in me. I find I don't mind the idea.

Martha fascinates me, actually. Usually she strikes me as scarcely older than I am, except that there's been more time in her life and therefore more has happened to her. But every so often a sort of gritty concrete wisdom flashes out from somewhere in the depths of her personality, surprising me, reminding me that I like older women.

I have heard Martha's story only in bits and pieces. The closeted adolescence in Indiana in the bad old days; getting fired from a teaching job because of a scandal involving some student; the desperate break, fleeing to New York with a car full of books and plants; the proverbial year alone in a fifth-floor walkup on the Lower East Side. She's gotten herself together over the years, now has a fairly well-paid job in publishing, and has begun to write more seriously—but it's been a slow process. And there are aches, old breaks, subtle cripplings that sometimes manifest themselves like ancient war injuries.

She alludes darkly to various short disastrous affairs, and at least one tragic true love. She takes loads of vitamins, smokes a pack of Trues a day, and worries about cancer.

The Homophobia in Media demo. It's a nice sunny day. We march around in a small circle on the sidewalk in front of the radio station carrying signs like WSWG IS A HETEROSEXIST PLOT and chanting slogans. The slogans, of which "Two, four, six, eight, gay is just as good as straight" is a representative example, are puerile and embarrassing, but after ten minutes of walking in that circle, I find I can get into yelling almost anything. The picket line consists of a few dykes and a wide assortment of faggots, from the handsome hip young in their blue jeans to the old-fashioned middle-aged in pancake makeup. There's a pleasantly anarchistic flavor to this event; we seem to be back in that brief portion of the sixties when, as I recall, the sun always blessed political protest and the college kids never worried too much about getting busted.

Suddenly Ellen materializes at the edge of the small crowd of spectators, looking like Pallas Athena just sprung from the head of Zeus or something. She's wearing a scoop-necked lavender leotard with jeans, keys on the left, a LESBIANS IGNITE button. I had thought she was still in Minneapolis.

We embrace formally, like heads of state at a summit conference. I can tell she's a bit nervous. She never did have K.L.'s nerve.

I take the offensive. "Will you have a cup of coffee with me?"

She looks rather relieved. *Ellen is a cold bitch,* I pronounce internally, just to fortify myself for anything that may follow.

So we drink coffee; we talk of Minneapolis. It's snowing there. Ellen has come out to her parents. I couldn't care less, and yet there's a certain fascination in talking to her. As with K.L. at the dance, I'm amazed at my own self-possession.

"I'm going to ask you a weird question," she says, fingering her keys. "I hope you don't mind. I absolutely need to know."

"Of course."

"Has K.L. talked to you about me?"

"Why should she?"

"I suppose I'm paranoid, but it occurred to me she might have decided to spread some venom through our particular corner of the women's community. My absence was a fine opportunity to get a head start on presenting her version, so to speak."

"Her version of what?"

"You didn't know that K.L. and I had a horrendous argument before I left?"

"Uh-uh."

"And that she's been sleeping with this woman Diane from the Karate Institute? I was sure it would be public information by now."

"Nobody ever tells me anything, it appears."

"It's funny," she says, "or rather, it's ironic. I guess I was more hung up on K.L. than I was aware of at the time."

Ellen herself taught me the truth of a remark she once made: "People are so damn three-dimensional." People in fact are like mountains. You get a very different perspective when you walk around and take a look from the other side. Ellen's asking me for something now, and of course I want to give it; but I remember my resolutions. I drink my cold coffee and murmur my distanced sympathy; with relief I watch her walk off in the direction of her train. It is, naturally, only when she's out of earshot that it dawns on me I've just missed my chance to follow Martha's advice and tell her off.

It occurred to me today that perhaps the world does not owe me sexual/emotional gratification. It was a radical thought: not particularly cheerful, but bracing at least, like the cold showers I may soon be reduced to taking. There are no guarantees. Like nobody really knows if Preparation H will shrink your hemorrhoids, or if the turbanned men with nose rings on the F train ever send your donations of small change to starving kids overseas.

"I'm through with sex!" I announce melodramatically, as if hurling defiance at the gods. Martha and I have just finished dinner. I'm sitting at one end of her dilapidated couch. She's sitting at the other, shoes off, hugging her knees to her chin. She looks small and very young.

"Nonsense," she says. "You cannot escape sex. It will track you to the ends of the earth."

We've been talking about dependence in relationships.

"Did you ever think you might be happier if you insisted *less* on your independence?" Martha asks, after an awkward silence.

"It's easy enough for you to say that," I snap. "You have no idea what a state I was in for at least two solid fucking months after Ellen and K.L. got together."

"You really think I don't?" That old therapeutic technique again: mirror the patient's statements. I wait, but Martha is stubborn.

"O.K., what's that supposed to mean?" I prod at last.

"You *really* don't understand?" She starts to laugh, looking at me.

"Why am I so funny?"

"Not you. The situation. It's hilarious. You really, really never realized that Ellen and I were lovers?"

I take a moment to consider. My mind's-eye contour map of emotional reality convulses, shifts dramatically. When I take time to look back, of course, I'll realize I should have known. Probably this will explain a lot of things.

"That fucker," I say, almost with admiration.

"But you know she's not trying to hurt any of us, not really," Martha chides gently.

"No, of course not. 'Why, what could she have done, being what she is?/Was there another Troy for her to burn?' and all that," I answer. "How long did it last?"

"A month at most. Right before she got involved with you you."

"Why did it end?"

"She told me a lot of different things. At one point I remember her saying, 'You're too attractive to me and that freaks me out. I'm scared of that kind of involvement.' But I think she came closer to the truth when she said, 'I don't think I can handle being with an older woman. It feels incestuous.' "

"My god, it must have been hard for you."

"Excruciating. But I survived to tell it."

I remember the emotional map. "Shit," I say. "Does this mean we can never really be alone?"

"You want to be alone?"

"No, I don't mean it like that. I mean alone together. You and me. Any of us. I was just thinking how tired I am of always reckoning on where the others are in this infernal web of relationships. The group dynamics seem so much more important than what happens between any two people. I feel paralyzed." What do I mean, what do I hear myself saying? Over and over again I've experienced this moment of indecision, when I'm not sure whether I'm about to stop talking theoretically or not.

But later, lying on Martha's couch because it's late and I can't afford a car service and the train is too dangerous and I have to work tomorrow—or these are the reasons Martha and I articulate for my staying—I begin to feel that I have not seen Martha before. That I have been looking through her, past her, all along.

Or is it that I've been seeing her objectively up to this point, and now the delusions begin?

I wake with a stiff neck. Martha is standing peering shortsightedly through the curtain, wearing her terrycloth robe, her fuzzy slippers muffling her feet. Her legs are really quite hairy. I've never noticed that before for some reason; my image of her has always been in pants and looking pressed and rather professional, dressed for work. She has a coffee mug in each hand.

"I think this is a two-pack day," she says, handing me my coffee.

"You mean you're going to smoke two packs?"

"No, I mean the atmosphere is going to do two packs' worth of damage to everyone's lungs before I smoke anything." She grimaces. She looks, in fact, terribly ratty, uncombed and vulnerable. I'm very glad to see her. I sit up, wrapping the blankets modestly around me. She sits at the foot of the couch, lights cigarettes, hands me one.

Now, smoking first thing in the morning has always seemed impossibly decadent to me, but with my eyes pasted into sockets stinging with lack of sleep I feel reckless and impossibly decadent anyway. So I take it.

"Did you sleep well?"

"Yes." Why do I lie incessantly just to get through my life?

"Not true. You have huge circles under your eyes."

"Well, a strange bed. . . ," I say.

"It felt a little funny to me, how we said goodnight last night," she says.

We're talking on two different levels. This time I decide to reply on the second, the more dangerous. "I wonder if it ever gets any better. It always seems so awkward, deciding what you want. I have to admit it was lots easier being straight, knowing the rules, not living with this ambiguity all the time."

"What do you mean?" she says, and for a minute I'm terrified she's going to go back to the first level and pretend the second doesn't exist. No way. I won't have it.

"What do you think I mean?" I say. "I'm not your bloody mother."

"Never mind what I think; I want to know what you mean."

This is arm-wrestling; this is Russian roulette. And we call ourselves mature women.

"That I think you're very beautiful," I say, looking right at her. And even as I say it I'm not sure what I mean, because it's completely unrehearsed.

I see her flinch the first moment; then she accepts it, accepts it. The coffee cup, the cigarette, all props are gone from her hands. She is floating toward me, smiling.

"Romance is dead," she says softly, lovingly, kissing me or not, depending.

The Warsaw Ghetto

wearing her long blue bathrobe mother ascends that hill. sirens soldiers dogs barking closer etc. face ravaged beyond hope but that you knew already it's part of the setup. bundle in her arms she holds out to me blanket soft child like a plastic explosive i want no part of this not even in dreams. . .

wake up six o'clock black square of window just turning grey. laurie breathing arm blue-veined on my pillow. trapped between wall and her beautiful muscled back i doze dodging nightmare.

kim kinetic rises new created each morning. channel changer click other side of wall television sound always through this life. wailing finger hurts wants breakfast etc. etc. wait says laurie. childhood what was it always waiting for the grownups to get up.

but just as laurie moves her hand cool over eight o'clock my shoulder just as with a light light pressure clench and relaxation of muscle she calls me just as i start to go under kim starts crying. mommy mommy mommy the cat scratched me. jesus fuck scream god i'm not even her mother but get that kid noise out of my hair but no. patience. it's hard being anybody a child too remember. honey i'll go this time.

back in bed safe with her hair her warmth her cunt wet the fact that she loves me i touch gentle but later knead the flesh knot like dough it swells tough resilient under my hand. morning-efficient clandestine wanting it fiercely. later cloudy as though through ether i see her bent serious as a midwife over me i struggle gasp grapple with this thing.

boundaries of skin vague we always fit better after. phone rings kim comes charging shouting i'll get it vaults over disordered limbs. hello this is kimberly wilson speaking may i ask who's calling. lapsing into vernacular oh hi grandma. she gets that bullshit from her sunday daddy answers like the girls do at his office.

daylight in the swamps i intone like father always did saturday mornings and rise shower kim crouching on toilet asking questions. nomi am i jewish? no you and laurie aren't jewish. why? because your relatives aren't jewish. they're irish german english dutch. is that what yours are too? no i'm jewish. do you say jewish pears? do i what? do you say jewish pears. like when you close your eyes and say pears to jesus.

breakfast. restaurant terribly crowded and we get the mean old waitress. don't call her that kim it's oppressive i admonish but she is anyway. platinum hair wrenched back to a pony tail rivets sagging masklike features to skeletal structure. lumps of fat jiggle on arms as she slams down coffee slopped in saucers and the wrong order. possible hangover probable righteous indignation as oppressed woman holding down shit job but also obvious contempt for two women no men a child than which there is no social grouping more déclassé. i child of bronx am calloused but laurie raised on long island objects to engaging in breakfast struggle. withhold tip i propose. intense theoretical discussion on issue of white working class follows.

kim suddenly demands bathroom threatens to pee on floor. two women blue hair hairnets opposite booth frown raise eyebrows murmur poor little boy his coat is torn. kim off to bathroom. tip. scowl at women. pay bill.

drive into city kim leaning over seat back kvetching into my ear laurie yelling. kim shutup you're giving me a headache finally i explode. mommy nomi wasn't nice to me she said something that wasn't nice told me to shut up my teacher says it isn't nice to say shutup predictably she howls. right on i say thank the goddess i don't live by your teacher's tightassed kindergarten standards of nicety meanwhile high we fly over brooklyn bridge water toward towers of manhattan thrust this morning into unnaturally clear air. whatever would we have done with you in the warsaw ghetto i groan. what's a warsaw ghetto kim stops bawling long enough to inquire.

kim laurie conclude separate peace stroll through sporting goods store holding hands. kim pretends to ignore me but if thoughts could kill i'd keel right over. bad vibes expedition a failure no suitable tents. laurie drops me off at train station we embrace public perfunctory grim. goodbye kim i say trying to look dignified indifferent. kim clamps hands over ears.

take train back to brooklyn read life in the iron mills. train stalls in tunnel fifteen minutes underwater between boroughs. shopping bag lady in next car expressing hysteria others keep to themselves jumps up shouting hurry train hurry train hurry train hurry.

stop on way home from station pick up cheese yogurt bean curd vegetables. arrive home find mail consists one final disconnect notice from gas company. living room piled with a week's worth of newspapers kim's train set one hideous charmin' charlotte doll books mail drafts of laurie's last article clothes clean and dirty. ignore objective conditions of existence.

landlord here for rent. how fortunate my extra shirt he won't notice my breasts. hassle about bathroom plumbing. he won't fix wants us to pay. well i don't know how soon we can have it taken care of and it's flooding downstairs i mention polite tough coping. thinking which judo move i'd lay him out with if he tried anything.

do a wash. mop up overflow. put wash in dryer. wash dishes. clean sink. punish cats for shitting behind couch. clean up shit. eat lunch. walk to park.

spring. forsythia. fever. that spurious weekend freedom. signs new-stencilled on mailboxes say fight for socialism. liberated fathers in droves wheel babies through park. cop car lurks by lake. kids tear flowers off trees. in april park changes like a clock hand moving imperceptibly day by day. trapped in offices under fluorescent lighting we don't see it.

think about scene with kim. so angry i was this morning and i don't even get credit for being the mother. you acted like a baby i could say vindictive but it would be inaccurate. it's a highly sophisticated technique she's developed really.

good thing about kids you learn self-sacrifice become a better person mother said. i never wanted a child but had an abortion when i was seventeen and there are no accidents. family affair doctor a colleague of my father's safe sterile almost painless very hush hush. they might have left me to backalley butchers they might have made me give it up i might have had stretchmarks. dumb luck that i didn't. they made me feel it.

but the process the fetus growing in me the mother that part never seemed tangible any more than adulthood years their passage the fact of death. because actually you can't choose to have kids they are all necessary or seem so at the time women not knowing how to prevent or conned into thinking it's what they want. men doing the convincing rendering us irrevocably dumb female chained is how i saw it.

my birth for example makes no sense i always felt my mother ought to have known better. for somewhere outside my childhood dressed in sober but well-tailored clothing of the period revealing her lovely figure my mother stands on the prow of a ship that glides past the statue of liberty. escape from wartorn europe is the drama there is nothing tired poor or wretched about her she'll learn to speak classier english than my father who kept his bronx accent always they glide glide past.

of course it didn't look like that and i wasn't there. half her family died anonymously in europe but she came here and after the war married my father. in '48 i was born proving nothing had been learned. when i was sixteen my favorite song was masters of war the line about fear to bring children into the world. they live in florida now and I'm reading simone de beauvoir on the coming of fascism. how all the left refused to believe see denied it but it happened anyway like death and taxes.

back home i sit at my desk fidget jot down worthless scraps of would-be poetry decide to start dinner. six o'clock news says kissinger like a manipulative father warning cuba stay out of africa. who asked him anyway. i'm missing laurie.

after dark they come i'm chopping salad vegetables rice cooking. laurie holds me tired she says she's going to lie down. kim oblivious of the morning's horrors stays behind wants to help. suggest she come to store with me get salad oil. tell her she can give the money herself. she runs eager for the adult experience of paying for something to get her coat.

nomi when i grow up how will i get money? her hand in mine. this is what i was talking about not wanting being a grownup socializing children explaining capitalism. kids aren't friends peers and the whole process of molding deciding how things should be is not what i like finally. you have to be too careful of your power.

i don't know kim i answer hoping to laugh it off maybe after the revolution you'll do meaningful labor. there are lots of ways for people to earn money i add optimistically. some places you don't need money to live people just make what they want and trade with each other. i'm not even sure that's anthropologically sound but i'd like it to be i'd like to be able to help her imagine it.

waiting in line watching her pointy face little under the floppy hat i try to fix it in my mind thinking in ten years when she's fifteen what will she be what will i remember. knowing still our lives aren't made that way. ten years and i could be anywhere the world could not be. it's what we live with.

man tells me how much for salad oil. i give money to kim she stretches up hands it to him. oh hi there little fellow he says adding jovial so long mom to me beaming selfsatisfaction getting it all wrong.

nomi why did he call me a little fellow that's a boy she asks me expecting answers. for the same reason he called me a mom because he doesn't know beans i say and she laughs squeezes my hand in solidarity we march sisters in struggle back up the block.

the hall is dark i fill her plate leave her to tv's tender mercies go tell laurie dinner. kim in her room we at table discuss laurie's great neck afternoon with folks. so many things i didn't understand about my family families before i had kim she says. think i should try i say. it could be a new kind of therapy have a child and come to terms with your past. but we've been doing it so long you never seem to get pregnant laurie says. maybe we're not doing it right i say. ever thought of parthenogenesis asks laurie kissing me across the table.

two little lovebirds sitting in a tree
k-i-s-s-i-n-g
first comes love
then comes marriage
then comes nomi with a baby carriage

chants kim pirouetting into our midst in startling drag her pink ballerina tutu. see this tutu nomi i'm going to show it to my daddy tomorrow he says i can be a ballerina when i grow up. but somehow the pirouettes keep turning into leaps jumps sprints miss their intended effect. i learned that rhyme in grade school myself the boys peeked under the girls' skirts when they climbed on the monkey bars. kim wears pants to school now you've come a long way baby they say.

completing evening ritual we carry kim to bed. laurie exhausted watches tv turns in early. i stay up late write letters climb into bed to find her out cold but warm in sleep she turns to me. over and over i come back to this like playing that billie holiday song they can't take that away from me this body love safety all of it. they can't in whatever universe take away that it was i believe wondering is that enough. wondering in fifty years will we look back on this from the wisdom clarity of the lesbian old age home having made it all the way to home base death in bed in fifty years will we look.

Daddy

I like my Daddy's best. It has more rooms. Mommy just has an apartment and you have to go upstairs. The bathroom is in my room. Daddy has two bathrooms. He owns the whole house. Mommy used to live there when I was a little baby. Before they got divorced. That means not married anymore. You get married when you love each other.

Mommy loves me. Daddy says I'm his favorite girl in the whole world, sugar. He always calls me sugar. We like to go to a restaurant for breakfast. Sometimes we go there for dinner if he has to work in the city. I went to his office lots of times. He has books there. You go way up in the elevator. Sometimes I feel like I'm going to throw up. But I don't. Then you see the river. There's no one there except Daddy and me. Sometimes Ellen comes.

My Mommy works. She goes to meetings. First I have to go to school and then daycare. You can make noise at daycare. At school you have to be quiet or you get punished. But I didn't ever get punished. Mommy helps me with my homework. Sometimes we read a book together. Daddy asks me add and take away. He says sugar you're so smart you can be anything you want to be when you grow up. A doctor or a lawyer or a professor or anything. My Daddy's a lawyer. I don't know if I'll get married.

Daddy said maybe next year I can go to a different school where they have lots of things to play with. You can paint and go on trips and they have nice books. The kids make so much noise in my class. Some of them talk Spanish and the boys are bad. I got a star for doing my homework right.

My Daddy takes me on Sunday. Sometimes I sleep there if Mommy goes away. I have to be good. Daddy says he'll get me something when we go shopping if I behave. I have to take a bath before I go and brush my hair. Daddy says he likes little girls that smell nice and clean. Sometimes Ellen lets me try her perfume. Once she let me put some powder on my face and some blue stuff on my eyes. That's eye shadow. But I had to wash my face before I went home. Mommy doesn't wear makeup. Or Carolyn. They said it looks silly.

Once in the summer I stayed at my Daddy's for a whole week. Ellen was there. She helped take care of me. You're so helpless David she said. She laughed. We all laughed. I had fun. We went to Coney Island. During the week I just call my Daddy two times because he works hard. Sometimes if he goes on a trip he can't see me. Daddy and Ellen went on a trip to Florida. They had to fly in an airplane. They sent me a postcard every day. You could go swimming in the winter there. Mommy and me went to the country but the car broke.

Sometimes Carolyn stays overnight. We only have two beds. She has to sleep in the same bed with Mommy. When I wake up I get in bed with them. We all hug each other. Carolyn and Mommy kiss each other all the time. But they aren't married. Only a man and a woman can get married. When they want to have a baby the man's penis gets bigger and he puts it in the woman's vagina. It feels good to touch your vagina. Me and Veronica did it in the bathtub. When the baby comes out the doctor has to cut the Mommy's vagina with some scissors. Mommy showed me a picture in her book.

I saw Daddy's penis before. Mommy has hair on her vagina. She has hair on her legs and Carolyn has lots of hair on her legs like a man. Ellen doesn't. Mommy said maybe Ellen does have hair on her legs but she shaves it. Sometimes I forget and call Carolyn Ellen. She gets mad. Sometimes I forget and call

Mommy Daddy. I have a cat called Meatball at Mommy's but sometimes I forget and call Meatball Max instead. That's Daddy's dog.

Daddy is all Jewish. So is Ellen. Mommy is only part Jewish. But Daddy said I could be Jewish if I want. You can't have Christmas if you're Jewish. Mommy and me had a little Christmas tree. Carolyn came. We made cookies. I had Chanukah at my Daddy's. He gave me a doll named Samantha that talks and a skateboard and green pants and a yellow top. He says when I learn to tell time he'll get me a watch.

I wish Mommy would get me a TV. I just have a little one. Sometimes it gets broken. Daddy has a color TV at his house. It has a thing with buttons you push to change the program. Mommy said I watch too much TV. I said if you get me a new TV I promise I'll only watch two programs every day. Mommy said we're not going to just throw things away and get a new one every year. I told her Andrea has a color TV in her house and Veronica has a nice big TV in her room that you can see good. Mommy said I'm not getting a TV and that's all. Mommy made me feel bad. I started crying. Mommy said go to your room you're spoiling my dinner. I said *asshole* to Mommy. That's a curse. Sometimes my Mommy says a curse to me. I cried and cried.

Mommy said get in your room. She spanked me and said now get in your room. I ran in my room and closed the door. Mommy hurts my feelings. She won't let me watch TV. She always goes to a meeting and I have to stay with the baby sitter. I don't say a curse to my Daddy. My Daddy isn't mean to me. I screamed and screamed for my Daddy and Mrs. Taylor next door got mad and banged on the wall.

Mommy said go in the other room and call him then. Daddy said you sound like you've been crying. What's the matter, sugar. Nothing I said. Daddy doesn't like me to cry. He says crying is for little babies. I can't stand to see a woman cry, sugar, he says. Then I laugh and he tells me blow my nose. What are we going to do on Sunday I said. Oh that's a surprise Daddy said. Is it going somewhere I said. Yes we're going somewhere but that's not the real surprise Daddy said.

Is it a present I said. Daddy said just wait and see, what did you do in school today. Daddy always asks what did I do in school. I told him the teacher had to punish Carlos. Daddy said listen isn't it about your bedtime. I have work to do. Ellen says hi. Blow me a goodnight kiss.

I hugged my Mommy. She hugged me back. She said she was sorry she got mad. But don't beg for things. A new TV is expensive. We don't need it. Mommy always says it's too expensive. I said I wish you were married to the President. Then we could live in the White House. I saw a picture in school. You could have anything you want. They don't have cockroaches.

The President is a good man. He helps people. George Washington was the President. Veronica gave me a doll of his wife at my birthday. It has a long dress. Mommy said he was mean to Indians and Black people. But we studied about him in school and he wasn't. They had voting once. You could vote for Ford or Carter. My Daddy voted for Carter. I'm glad my Daddy voted for who won. My Mommy didn't vote.

Mommy doesn't like things. She doesn't like the President and she doesn't like Mary Hartman like my Daddy. I told her to get Charmin toilet paper like they have on TV because it's soft to squeeze. She said that's a rip-off. She only takes me to McDonald's once every month. I got a Ronald McDonald cup to drink my milk. She said that's a gimmick. I like milk. Milk is a natural. I told Mommy that and she got mad. I said you don't like anything Mommy. She said I like lots of things. I like plants. I like to play basketball. I like sleeping late on Sunday mornings. I like to eat. I like books. I like women. I like you.

Do you like men I said. I don't like most men very much Mommy said. Some men are okay. My Daddy likes women I said. Does he Mommy said.

I asked my Daddy does he like women. He said extremely. Some of my favorite people are women he said. Like you. And Ellen. Why do you ask. I said I don't know. Daddy said do you like men. I love you Daddy I said. I bet she gets that you know where Ellen said.

On Sunday we had breakfast at my Daddy's house. We had pancakes. Daddy makes them. He puts on his cook's hat. Then we went shopping. Then we went to a movie of Cinderella. Ellen came too. Then we went to a restaurant. I had ice cream with chocolate. Ellen and Daddy held each other's hand. Daddy said now I'm going to tell you the surprise. Ellen and I are getting married. How does that sound, sugar. Ellen said for god's sake David give her a little time to react.

Daddy said I can be in the wedding. He said Ellen will wear a pretty dress and he will break a glass. He did that when he and Mommy got married too. Then Ellen will have the same name as Mommy and Daddy and me and I can call her Mommy too if I want. I won't have to see my Daddy just on Sunday because Ellen will be there to help take care of me. She only works in the morning. It will be like a real family with a Mommy and a Daddy and a kid. But I can't say that part because Daddy said it's supposed to still be a secret.

I didn't feel good when Daddy brought me home. I felt like I had to throw up. Mommy held my hand. I lay down on the bed and she brought Meatball to play with me. She asked what did I do with Daddy today. She always asks me that. I told her we saw Cinderella. It was okay. She rode in a pumpkin. Some parts were boring. The Prince loved her. Daddy and Ellen are going to get married.

I started crying. I cried hard. Then I had to throw up. It got on the rug.

Mommy got the washcloth. She brought my pajamas. She hugged me. She said I love you. She said it won't be so different when Daddy and Ellen are married. You like Ellen don't you.

I love you Mommy, I love you, I love you I said. Why don't you like my Daddy. I love my Daddy.

I don't dislike your father Mommy said. We don't have much in common that's all. I'm happy living here just with you. You're special to me and you're special to your Daddy. You see him every week.

I cried and cried. I love you Mommy. I love you and Daddy both the same. And I love Ellen because she's going to be my Mommy too. I'll miss you. I'll miss you so much when I live there. I'll cry. I'm going to have a big sunny room and Daddy said he'll paint it and I can pick a color. I'm going to have a new kitty so I won't miss Meatball. Next year I can go to that nice school and Ellen might have a baby. It would be a brother or a sister. Daddy's going to get me a bicycle. I can take anything there I want. I'll just leave a few toys here for when I come to visit you on Sunday.

Children's Liberation

You know it is summer because she is wearing a tube top the color of those violent pink artificially flavored ices you buy in pizza stores and a pair of navy blue shorts that probably fit last year. She has dark hair and brown eyes and skinny, scarred brown legs, and in this context you might reasonably assume her to be Puerto Rican, though in fact she is half Italian and half something else she can never remember, not having seen her father since she was four years old. She is sitting on a rubber tire in the middle of a rubble-strewn lot.

Before her stretches a desert vista of half-cleared blocks, interrupted in the distance by a residential street. To her left are some fire-gutted apartment buildings which their owner, the city, has neglected either to tear down or board up; to her right is the mural project. Behind her is Brooklyn, a habit, a tropical nightmare she takes for reality, a street of heat and heroin, ailanthus, open hydrants, and women in advanced stages of pregnancy pushing strollers. The sun is a yellowish stain soaking through the smog; the air tastes of metal. She takes for granted her clogged nose, the hair lying wet and heavy on her neck. Adults may squint up at the sky and talk about rain. Children endure.

Been on a train
And I'm never gonna be the same

she sings to herself. She is going to be a musician someday, which is even more exciting than being a painter.

She's been visiting the mural site ever since the scaffolding went up. It has taken several weeks for the panorama of faces, fists and bright flags to transfigure what had been an ordinary brick wall. Today they are painting the apex of the design, the World Trade Center with a banner reading, "Viva Puerto Rico Libre!" unfurling from the top. It is not the mural itself, however, but the purposefulness and camaraderie of the painters, most of them high school Youth Corps workers, which really attracts her. She is enchanted by their casual horseplay on the scaffold, their skill in transferring an image from a four-by-seven color sketch to a four-story wall. She has made no effort to talk to any of them.

But now for the first time someone approaches her, no high school student but a grown man with paint-stained jeans and tufts of paint in his afro. His salutation startles her. She had counted on not being noticed.

"You live around here?"

She nods a reluctant "uh-huh," concentrating on a pattern she is making in the dirt with the toe of her sandal.

"Here on the block?"

"No."

"Where, then?"

"Up near the Park."

"Oh, up near the Park. The Park," he repeats. "It's real nice up there. Clean streets."

She looks up at him now, having almost anticipated but still not quite understanding the sarcasm in his voice. She is in a hurry to figure out what he wants so she can give it to him and make him go away.

"What street, up near the Park?"

"Twelfth Street."

"Twelfth Street? And you come all the way down here every day to watch some people paint pictures on a wall?"

Actually he is impressed, now, but she misinterprets the remark as a further reproach. "It's not so far," she says defensively.

"Your mother work?"

"She goes to school. Welfare sends her."

"But she knows you come down here?"

"Sure. She doesn't care." She still doesn't know what he wants.

"I've been watching you sitting there every day. I thought maybe you'd like to help us paint."

"Maybe," she says reluctantly, playing for time. Nervously she twists the keys strung around her neck.

"Maybe? You can't give me any better than a maybe? I was going to say, if you come tomorrow you could help paint down there in the left-hand corner. That woman's face. We can't let you up on the scaffold, but there's plenty to finish on the ground." He waits.

"That would be okay," she answers, understanding finally what he wants. "Thank you."

"Fine, that's great, it's a deal then, see you tomorrow." Smiling as if he'd just given her a present, he goes back to work.

Angry and depressed, she gets up to leave. The vacant lot with its bustle of legitimate activity from the street and the mural was perfect, and he has ruined it for her. She will never be able to come back now, at least not until the mural is finished. And she can't go to the Park anymore. She used to hang out there at the beginning of the summer. But then she began hearing stories, getting nervous, thinking creepy people might be hiding in the woods. Finally one morning a woman's body was found dumped in the lake.

It's only three-fifteen according to the clock on the Williamsburgh Savings Bank tower. Not time to go home yet. More than any other time of day she hates midafternoon, hates returning then to the stuffy empty apartment where bored, lethargic cats greet you in the hall, not understanding that you too are bored, lonely and hot. She hates the posters shouting slogans from the walls everywhere except in her own room, which is not really even hers because you have to walk through it to get to Chris's room. No, she would rather loiter along Fifth Avenue as though on an errand for her mother, peering into the dark cluttered windows of bodegas, daring herself to snatch an apple from the display outside the Korean vegetable store.

In fact, she now recalls, she is supposed to pick up a quart of milk; she has a whole dollar in her pocket and could stop for something.

Now she is comfortably inconspicuous again because she has nothing anybody wants, though in a few years walking the same street wearing the same shorts and brief top she will occasion innumerable murmured propositions, hissed obscenities.

You've got more tracks on you mister
Than the tracks on this train

she begins humming again, prompted by the sight of the knots of idle men jamming each sidewalk corner and spilling over into the intersection. The street is famous for dope traffic; in fact, she has heard that a baby carriage parked in front of a certain laundromat means they're selling stuff there that day.

She passes a laundromat. Outside the women stand, waiting for their washing to get done, for clothes get dirty and have to be washed even in the middle of a heat wave. Sure enough, there's a baby carriage with a baby asleep in it. She wonders if this is *the* laundromat, *the* baby carriage. Would whoever it is really use a carriage with a real live baby? It seems wrong somehow. She wonders how a needle stuck into your arm can feel good, and which of the men she passes, averting her eyes slightly because already she know better than to look directly at them, is a junkie. Her father was a junkie too, or she thinks so; Chris has hinted at this in certain unguarded moments, mainly during fights.

I saw a man
Take a needle full of hard drugs
And die slow

she sings, feeling better now, in love with the energy of despair behind that song, in love with the life of the street, the rotten city's vitality, the women clustered on stoops. She envies them their rootedness, language, the Puerto Rican Spanish and Haitian French they speak with authority and fantastic speed, the babies they rock in carriages.

"Comidas Latinas y Chinas": this is the sign by which she recognizes the restaurant she's been looking for. She used to be taken here regularly in the years before she was old enough to stay alone. It would be very late at night following some meeting or other; she would be sleepy and irritable and fed up with the haphazard system of rotating childcare to which she'd invariably been relegated. Chris and the others would just keep talking, clicking off the familiar phrases like rosary beads: contradiction, exploitation, struggle. But they would eat chicken fried rice, and that she liked.

The restaurant is cool, empty except for a few people sitting up at the counter. She has hardly ever been in a restaurant alone before, and feels nervous ordering. But the Chinese waiter doesn't even blink when she says "cafe con leche" a little quickly, a little loudly, afraid perhaps he'll ask to see her money or tell her little girls shouldn't drink coffee. And in fact she has always hated coffee, beverage of grownups, but now she sits there comfortably drinking it. For a few minutes she is happy, wrapped in childhood like a cloak of invisibility, free, not accountable to anyone.

Tell me why love is like
Just like a baaaaaalll
And chain

Hearing the music all the way out in the street, Chris knows it's coming from her apartment. Lisa's on this music kick lately, says she wants to be a singer when she grows up. She has resurrected all of Chris's least favorite records—these include, for example, the Stones, Cream and the Grateful Dead—from a box in the back of a closet. She has begged for piano lessons, hoping someday to accompany herself like Laura Nyro. But Chris remembers hours of enforced piano practice, her own mother working at a luncheonette to pay for the hated lessons; she is not about to sacrifice to what she calls Lisa's bourgeois aspirations.

The apartment, three flights up, is hotter than the street. "Turn that fucking masochistic heterosexual noise down," Chris hollers on her way into the kitchen, where she discovers the carton of milk, purchased two hours ago and warm now, sitting out on the counter in a paper bag.

Lisa appears, lounges in the kitchen doorway, long-limbed and dirty-faced. The record's still blasting away.

"What's for dinner?"

"Cold bean salad."

"Yuk."

"Lisa, I asked you to turn the record down. And I told you day before yesterday and last week and a million times before that, put the milk in the refrigerator. It goes bad. It's not like we have money to throw away."

"I want a grilled cheese sandwich."

"Make it yourself, then. Take care of the record first."

"You don't have to start yelling the minute you walk in the door."

Glaring, they sit down at the table. They might be ill-matched roommates, siblings rubbing each other the wrong way. It had been different when Lisa was little; they were closer then.

"When's school going to be over? It's boring when you're always gone," Lisa says finally.

"I'm sorry, babe. You know I'd be working if I wasn't in school."

"Eileen's mother stays home."

"Eileen's father works."

"You could get married."

There it is again, Lisa's solution to every human ill: get married. Stubbornly she continues to trot it out, though she's perfectly aware of Chris's position. When, several years ago, Chris announced she was a lesbian, Lisa's instant comeback was, "I'm not." Chris's friends were amused by the story and sure Lisa would outgrow it, but so far the kid remains passionately supportive of everything heterosexual: rock music, romantic movies, her grandmother's tales of church weddings and babies being born. And yet she's tough as nails; as Marcie says, there's not a femme bone in her body.

Of course this is all Lisa's business; "her karma," Chris once would have put it. Lisa may do as she pleases, at least so long as her actions affect only Lisa. Among the many posters which Lisa does not like because they symbolize Chris's violent, unreasonable opposition to the status quo, one on the kitchen wall proclaims: "Children's Liberation!"

"Christ, Lisa, you sound like my mother. Do we have to go over this again? You know I'm not getting married," Chris remonstrates now.

"Oh for god's sake. Other people's mothers aren't lesbians. Why do I have to have a fucking lesbian for a mother," Lisa bursts out.

"Wanting kids has nothing to do with being a lesbian or not."

"But you didn't want me, Chris. You even said." At times like this Lisa seizes any weapon.

"You know I never said I didn't want you. I always wanted a baby. I just didn't plan to get pregnant so soon, that's all. I was young, I was eighteen."

"Well, people ought to think before they do a thing like that," Lisa insists. "It's not like playing with dolls. It's serious."

"Most people who have babies don't have the faintest idea what they're doing. Don't feel so sorry for yourself."

"And if you had to have me, you should have stayed with my father." Lisa is inexorable. And has now gone too far.

"Oh, your father. Your father and beans and rice and food stamps and no money for the doctor and roaches hatching in the stove and him doing up in the bathroom and me sitting on a bench in Washington Square Park with you in a stroller and so fucked up on acid I couldn't figure out how to get home—no, I don't think I should have stayed with your father."

"Grownups should think what the hell they're doing," Lisa reiterates, starting to cry now but unsoftened by tears.

"Hey, I'm not putting up with this shit. You can stay here and cry and carry on and talk to yourself all night if you want. I'm going over to Marcie's."

"You promised you weren't. You promised."

"I did not promise. I said probably. That was before you started in."

"You're always going over there."

"Oh quit guilt-tripping me. You're big now. You don't need me every minute."

Chris goes into the bedroom, starts stuffing a change of clothes into her knapsack. Lisa follows, wailing, "Chris, you promised."

"I did not promise."

"You did so."

"Look, you can ask Eileen up if you want. Just don't play the music too loud. You can call me if there's anything important. I'll be back in the morning on my way to school."

"Mother!" Lisa screams; it is the ultimate appeal. "Mother, I'll kill myself, I'll kill you, Mother."

Chris, who refuses to be manipulated by such references to their ancient relationship, reflects on the stairs that the one advantage in living in an apartment full of wife- and child-beaters is that a scene like this is not going to startle the neighbors. But she is not entirely unmoved by what she calls "Lisa's theatrics," for later she sits at Marcie's kitchen table, talking about it to Marcie and her two roommates.

"Sometimes I get this awful vision," she says. "Little apartments all over the city, single mothers trapped in there with their kids, like some torture where people are shut up with rats. Except in this case it's mutual."

"Isn't there any place Lisa could stay, even for just a little while, to give you a vacation?" one of the roommates sensibly suggests.

"Oh, my mother would love to get her hands on Lisa. But I wouldn't do that. I've lived with the woman myself."

Alone in the apartment, Lisa tries to think, finds she cannot. Nor can she hang onto her fear, her desperate sense of having been abandoned. Instead, she is flooded with a tremendous energy, a confidence which she does not quite know how to use. She is possessed by a few large, simple emotions: anger, the urge to flee.

Still, she is practical enough to remember she'll need money. In the kitchen cupboard is a sugar bowl in which Chris keeps cash for food and household supplies. Lisa has been pinching change from there for years, though Chris always says, "Ask, honey, and if I have the money I'll give it to you." Now she takes what she finds, a ten and several ones. There are subway slugs on top of Chris's bureau. Hot as it is, she snatches up a sweater on her way out.

She closes but does not lock the door, hurries the three and a half blocks to the subway. She can hardly believe that this could be so simple, yet once there her luck holds: the slug drops smoothly into the slot, the heavy revolving door turns without incident. Arbitrarily she picks the Manhattan-bound platform.

Lisa has never before been alone at night in a train station. The cavernous place, hospitable as a bomb shelter, seems even darker than usual; they've unscrewed half the light bulbs to save the city's money. The platform is nearly empty. She hunches against a pillar, hoping not to be noticed.

Finally the train comes. It is one of those new ones, air-conditioned, with orange, yellow and red seats. She is reassured by the familiar ads with their pictures of streams, forests and cigarette-smoking couples; by Miss Subways with her processed hair. Prudently she looks around for crazy people and teenage boys and, finding none, selects an outside seat in the middle of the car. Now she really must think.

She thinks all the way to Jamaica, Queens; all the way back down through Manhattan and Brooklyn to Coney Island; all the way back to Jamaica again. She imagines all the cities she could run away to if she had more money. She could even hitchhike to the west coast and find her father. If she were only a little taller, had breasts, she could hustle in Times Square.

By the second trip to Queens she has admitted to herself that these are not practical solutions. By the time they hit Coney Island again, she has made up her mind, resigned herself, draped her sweater over her shoulders to ward off the chill of the air conditioning, and curled up on the seat.

About three o'clock in the morning it occurs to a transit cop that this is a bad hour for a small white female child to be asleep in an otherwise empty car. He shakes her, rather gently for a cop.

"You lost, little girl?"

"No," she says immediately. Then, opening her eyes and seeing the uniform, she understands that he can make it easy. "Yes, I mean," she says without emotion.

"How'd you manage that?"

"I don't know."

The transit cop, though irritated by her self-possession, abides by his duty.

"Do you know where you live?"

"Of course. I live with Grandma."

They are in Brooklyn again. She gives him the phone number, and at Jay Street they get out and he makes the call.

"Something funny going on here," he mentions, handing her over to the regular cop in the squad car. "This grandmother didn't sound like the kid was expected. Check it out when you get there."

Lisa's grandmother, who lives in an old brick apartment building in Flatbush, is a tough woman. She has reared five children, outlived a difficult husband, managed to attain some small degree of economic security. Her hair is not even grey yet. Now she stands behind the glass coldly watching the two of them mount the steps: her granddaughter, accompanied by an officer of the law. Grudgingly, at last, she opens the door.

"Grandma, I want to stay with you," Lisa hurriedly announces.

"It's four o'clock in the morning. Where is your mother?"

"She's not home. I said I want to live here with you."

"Look, lady, make up your mind. Does this kid live here or not?" the cop starts in.

"You'd better leave her here," Lisa's grandmother replies, having sense enough at least to recognize the common enemy. "If you take her home I guarantee you won't find her mother. She goes out at all hours and leaves this girl totally unsupervised."

"Yeah, how'm I supposed to make sense of all this," the cop grumbles. But leaves.

Lisa waits now, confidently, to be admitted. But her grandmother still bars the door. She is accustomed to driving hard bargains, and has waited a long time for her chance at this one.

"You understand that if you live with me it won't be anything like it is at your mother's? You'll behave. You'll go to mass with me. You'll quit your swearing and lying and disobedience. I'll send you to Sacred Heart when school opens."

Lisa sighs, appearing for the sake of form to hesitate. In fact, she has thought it out already; without exactly knowing, she's been thinking it out for weeks. There is no stereo in her grandmother's apartment. On the other hand, there is a piano. Perhaps there will be money for music lessons. After all, it's a matter of endurance, and Lisa knows all about that. She's ten going on eleven now, already more than halfway to her eighteenth birthday.

Blood/Milk

The party in honor of Nadine Grossman's book—not the regular publication party, I mean, but the alternative feminist version—was held in a loft in Manhattan. Getting there was a hassle; I don't know any painters and usually manage to lose my way when I venture into the nest of ill-lit, underpopulated streets that is SoHo. Besides, it was a blustery November night. If I hadn't had to pay a baby sitter, I might have considered taking a cab; as it was, I ended up walking five blocks from the nearest IRT stop. Every so often a ragged figure would lurch out from a shadowy recess muttering a demand for something, sex or money, at which point I would clutch my shoulder bag more firmly, walk faster, and remind myself that drunks make weak assailants and in any event I know judo.

But capitalism is irrational. Upstairs, all was Burgundy and Brie, foliage and careful lighting, high ceilings and exposed brick, Cris Williamson on the stereo, Judy Chicago on the walls. The place was immense and beautifully renovated, with color-coordinated built-in kitchen appliances and several spacious loft beds. Any traces of artistic activity had been carefully concealed. I congratulated myself on my timing. The guest of honor was nowhere in evidence; I'd be able to drink a glass or two of wine before facing Nadine.

Two weeks prior to this fateful evening, my habitually optimistic anticipation of the daily mail had been rewarded by the arrival of a heavy, square envelope post-marked San Francisco. Inside was a printed card reading, "You are cordially invited to participate in a celebration of womanenergy upon the occasion of the publication of Nadine Grossman's book, *Blood/Milk*." Underneath, scribbled in the nearly illegible handwriting with which Nadine used to cover the pages of the school exercise books she used for diaries, was the message, "Do come if you possibly can. I'm dying to talk to you while I'm in N.Y.C. P.S. I love your poems!!!!"

My initial instinctive pleasure lasted about five seconds and was replaced by suspicion. Nadine and I hadn't communicated in at least five years; I had thought, before I stopped thinking about her much, that we would never speak again. Nevertheless, I did not seriously consider skipping the party. Instead, I squandered $9.95 on a copy of *Blood/Milk* the minute the hardback edition hit the stores, finishing it before the *Times* ran its atrociously distorting, sneakily homophobic review. I spent long hours going over obscure details of my past. I even threw the I Ching. Preparedness, I told myself, was the key.

Now, however, trapped in the high bright space of the loft which afforded no cover, I felt less confident about our imminent encounter. Many of the faces surrounding me were familiar, but they were not the faces of friends. This was a literary event with a vengeance; a gathering organized, so far as I could see, strictly for display purposes.

I abhor passive suffering, so I armed myself with a glass of wine and a dab of chopped liver on a cracker and began looking for someone to talk to. Across the room I spotted Frances Fairchild, lesbian-feminist-editor-about-town. We have one of those weird "professional" relationships kept alive mainly because we keep running into each other at poetry readings. She stood poised for flight, a bird of prey about to swoop down on the gathering and appropriate some useful piece of literary gossip. I intercepted her.

"I knew I shouldn't have come," she exclaimed eagerly. "Isn't it just ghastly?"

"On the whole, I think it looks quite civilized," I replied. With Frances one tries to provide balance.

"Oh definitely. Much too. That's just what I mean; the fangs are so skillfully concealed. I feel a whole lot safer when I can see them," she grimaced.

"What brings you here then?" I challenged.

"And talk about *heavies*," she continued, oblivious. "The place is so full of heavies we'll be lucky if the floor doesn't collapse before the evening's over."

This was uttered too loudly for my taste; barely ten feet away, one of the nation's most influential lesbian feminist poets was earnestly conversing with one of the nation's most influential straight feminist poets. "Why did you come?" I reiterated.

"Oh, because it's there, you know," said Frances impatiently.

"When's the anthology coming out?"

"January, I hope. We're having a hassle with the printer." Frances' eyes kept busy roving around the room; sometimes she even swivelled her head in the direction of the door, as people do in bars. Anyone who didn't know her might have thought she was looking for someone in particular.

"And what brings you here?" she inquired more politely at last.

"I'm an old friend of the author's."

"Of the *author's*? Of *Nadine Grossman's*?" Here, finally, was a topic calculated to hold Frances' interest.

"I knew her a long time ago, in my swinging bisexual days. We lived together in Seattle once."

"You were. . . involved?"

"You might call it that. Oh, it was quite a kinky scene, as they say. We were both very confused. It didn't work out at all." I had planned to be discreet; for the sake of my own dignity I had vowed not to discuss this with anyone.

"How long ago was all this?"

" '68, '69. We parted on awful terms; we haven't even written since I moved east."

"But I gathered from *Blood/Milk*. . . I mean, I thought she was with her husband a good deal later than that."

"She was, off and on. She used to take vacations, though, and I was one of her vacations. Her youngest daughter lived with us."

"Her husband must have been a tolerant guy."

"Oh, he was the original hip cool loose professor. Not really, of course, but on the surface. It was the late sixties, remember."

"Yes, the late sixties," Frances repeated knowingly, but I could see she was still recovering from the shock of finding out that I had been on such intimate terms with the author of *Blood/Milk*.

"Well, how do you feel about it?" she prompted after a minute.

"About what?"

"About all this. Her, the book. I mean, I hope I'm not offending you when I say the book appalled me. Not that she isn't talented."

"What appalled you about it?"

"Well, I *hate* the word 'confessional,' I mean I *never* use it, but I just can't think of any other way to describe that book. And *politically*—"

"You have to make a few compromises to publish with Random House," I couldn't resist remarking.

"Aha, you're jealous," Frances pounced. "Well, don't worry, it's nothing to be ashamed of. So are a lot of other women in this room."

"Oh, I don't care about Random House," I amended, not quite truthfully perhaps. "And I don't think *Blood/Milk* is as good as it could have been, but that's not the point either." I stopped to pour another glass of wine; I was beginning to enjoy myself. "What kills me, though, is the way she's managed to turn herself completely around in the space of a few years. I mean, there was nobody more anti-establishment than Nadine. We lived on food stamps. She volunteered on a radical newspaper. She used to stand in front of supermarkets *giving away* mimeographed copies of her poems, for Christ's sake."

"And you're still starving," Frances said succinctly.

"No, not starving. But still stuck with shitty office jobs and still struggling damn hard for each little ten-line poem I get printed in some magazine with a thousand circulation."

"So what do you think of Grossman's work?" Frances' tone was such that I half expected her to whip out pad and pencil and begin taking notes. I felt that anything I said might be used against me, but I had gone too far to quit.

"To begin with, I'm suspicious of diaries intended for publication. I'm not sure it's an honest concept, and I think it ends up violating the privacy of the other people in the author's life. Nadine always loved drama and self-revelation, and she knew how to use them to create an illusion of intimacy. I think she does the same thing in *Blood/Milk*."

"She's exhibitionistic," Frances summarized.

"On the other hand, I think she does wonderful stuff nobody else can do," I said. "I mean, she gives you that feeling of what life is really like sometimes, how anger and sexual frustration and jealousy really feel. All the big bad emotions she's very good at."

"But she's self-indulgent," Frances objected.

"I guess you could put it that way. I will say I've gotten very tired of her anti-craft pose. We always argued about that. She used to make fun of me for reading Henry James."

Nervously—Nadine certainly ought to have arrived by this time—I paused to survey the room. Frances' attention wavered; no longer able to repress her conviction that she was missing some exciting piece of the action, she saluted abruptly and sped off into the crowd, leaving me rather foolishly hoping she'd wait for another occasion to broadcast my critique. The party was in full swing: the great and the near-great—two National Book Award winners, one playwright who'd had something on Broadway the previous season, and the editors of several influential major press anthologies—mingled democratically with a substantial middle class of academics, critics and magazine editors, and a proletariat of women who, like myself, had once had a poem accepted by *Ms.* There I stood amid a barrage of conversation fragments: "And then my chairperson says to me, if you don't have any publications, could you at least give us some rejection slips for your file?" "If you rule out separatism as a strategy. . . " "Well, we already know we've got to go beyond Engels."

I began to think maybe Nadine wouldn't show. How exactly like her to have drunk too much, picked up someone in a bar. She could be in New Jersey at this very minute, and I'd be off the hook. It would probably be for the best. After all, what were we going to talk about? We had been together once, but we were someplace else now, someplace even Nadine, who was nine years my senior and ought to have been wise, had probably never anticipated.

Her rather dramatic entrance cut short this reverie. "My god, I'm sorry to be so late, I got lost, I had to take a cab from 96th and Broadway. . . " She was dressed in a sort of San Francisco-baroque second-hand shop fashion, very funky and un-New York, but much more elaborate than in the old days, when both our wardrobes had run heavily to men's cotton shirts. What shocked me after the first thirty seconds was the banality of actually being in the same room with her again.

Of course she was immediately surrounded by a congratulatory throng, and since I didn't feel like standing around with a million other people waiting to be noticed, I went to the bathroom. There I remained somewhat longer than necessary, trying to figure out what the hell I could say to her about *Blood/Milk*. The only solution I came up with was to drink some more.

Back at the wine I ran into my friend Jennifer, who works on a local feminist paper. "What are you doing here?" I asked her.

"I'm laughing," said Jennifer, who wasn't. "I'm laughing myself sick looking at all the funny people. You name it, they're here. Dyke academics ready to sell their souls for tenure in the women's studies department, small press publishers panting to be snapped up by the boys, marxist feminists who rake in twenty thou a year. Did you notice even Carole McNaughton's here? It's hilarious." She jerked her thumb over her shoulder. A woman standing with her back to me wearing riding boots, skintight jeans, keys on her belt, greying hair cropped to about a half inch all over her head, was unmistakeably Carole McNaughton, famous on the feminist lecture circuit for her militant, not to say authoritarian, advocacy of a separatist women's culture.

"I'll be damned," I said.

"Mark my words," Jennifer said, "the only reason Nadine Grossman can get away with this is because she isn't from New York. Publishing with Random House and being on good terms with Carole. It's a bit much."

"Well, Carole is a practical politician for all her talk," I pointed out. "What does she have to gain from boycotting Nadine? The damage is already done."

"But have you seen the ads for *Blood/Milk*? 'One woman's painfully honest record of her journey to another kind of love.' It's so *sick*!" Jennifer moaned.

"I know, I've seen everything," I replied.

At this moment Nadine noticed me.

She was less effusive than I'd expected. I introduced Jennifer, who fled with unwonted and not particularly welcome discretion. "Well, it's been awhile," said Nadine, mildly ironic, taking both my hands. "You look wonderful."

She exaggerated. A woman who lives alone with a three-year-old; who works as a secretary in midtown; who receives one hundred dollars a month child support; who does not have a lover, or a book out, or a grant from the state arts council—such a woman does not look wonderful. Nadine, on the other hand, though she did look older, looked also more vital, vibrant, infinitely more rested than I remembered.

"You look fine, too. You look so West Coast I can hardly stand it," I said.

"How?"

"Oh, I don't know. It's partly what you're wearing. And you look so healthy."

"Healthy!" hooted Nadine. "Physically, maybe. Emotionally. . . it's been a time of upheavals. But I won't go into that; I'm supposed to be on vacation."

"I enjoyed your book very much," I said, to get it over with. This was a blatant lie. I had experienced many emotions while reading *Blood/Milk*: fascination, envy, admiration, disgust, anger, all of them much more brutal and serious than enjoyment.

"Oh, did you? That makes me very happy," she said, as though she meant it, and I remembered how important it had always been to her to have everyone's approval. It wasn't enough for her that *Blood/Milk* was going to make her rich and famous. She cared what I felt.

"I suppose I was a bit put off by your decision to go commercial," I qualified.

"For what reason?"

"For one thing, look at the ads they're doing."

"Oh, they're disgusting, of course. But you have to expect that. The only thing that really matters is what's in the book, and the number of women it will reach," Nadine parried deftly. Of course, she must have been through this argument before.

"I'm not so sure; I think the medium is part of the message. When a feminist publishes with a commercial press, it just reinforces the idea that in order to be worth listening to, Random House has to publish you."

"You can't be too pure. All women simply don't have access to small press books. It's a class thing."

"All women don't have $9.95," I said rather irritably.

"When it comes out in paper, it'll be cheaper than if any of the women's presses had done it."

I resisted my impulse to ask about the movie rights, and instead remarked that of course I thought it was a decision every writer must make for herself.

"You think I'm inconsistent," said Nadine, who knew the uses of honesty.

I shrugged.

"I was living in real isolation before," she said. "We all were, before the Movement. My basic instincts were right, but I didn't have the slightest idea how to apply them. Besides, there's the money. I've been living hand to mouth ever since I left David. Only the privileged can afford the luxury of their idealism, you know."

I said I supposed that was true, and though I immediately thought of several counter-examples I didn't mention them.

"By the way, I really do admire your poetry. I saw the thing in *Ms*; I've seen some other stuff around," Nadine said. "Do you have a manuscript?"

"I've been thinking about putting one together, but frankly I don't know what I'd do with it."

"You should let me know when it's ready. I might be able to do something. I've got a very good agent."

I lashed myself to the mast, figuratively speaking; but it was too late. Once you've heard the sirens singing (and who doesn't, eventually?), they're bound to repeat on you, usually in the middle of some sleepless summer night when the humidity and the temperature are both way up in the nineties and your resistance is low.

To change the subject, I asked about the kids. Nadine, who clearly didn't want to talk about them, replied that they were fine, she saw them very infrequently, didn't get up to Seattle that often. "They even have a word for me now, I'm a 'drop-out mother,' " she said, laughing ruefully.

She surprised me. Even after reading her book I had not quite been able to believe she'd actually changed. Always she had been Nadine the mother; Nadine the creative sensitive mother who did it all; Nadine the hippie wife child servant hostess mother, cooking dinners, cooking dinners for fifteen people, getting the lovers to come to her because she couldn't leave the babies. And even when she left all that, came to me, it was with a baby strapped to her back. I found it difficult to believe that her many contradictions had at last come to rest in the person of this child-free woman with greying hair, Nadine Grossman the lesbian writer, the author of *Blood/Milk*.

"It's strange to meet here," I said lamely, feeling the need to remark on the strangeness of something since everything seemed so strange. "Do you remember how afraid I used to be to tell anyone I was a writer? I don't think either of us imagined we could have even part of what we wanted."

But apparently Nadine didn't want to consider such ironies. Instead she asked about my daughter, fumbling the name.

"Erika? She's fine. Fat and sassy. More passive and compliant than I'd like in some ways, which worries me."

"You really are a mother!" Nadine exclaimed delightedly, as though I had said something unbearably quaint.

Just as I was beginning to wonder how long I could stand the strain of further conversation, a woman wearing a leotard flung herself into the center of the room and began banging a small brass gong. "Oh, they must be starting the ritual," Nadine observed.

"Ritual?"

"The woman who organized this party said she wanted to have a ritual to celebrate the book. I told her I'd try anything once. You won't leave before we have a chance to talk some more, will you?"

I began looking for a suitable hideout. I've had experiences with rituals before. Finally I climbed into one of the loft beds, where I found Jennifer already comfortably ensconced with a generous supply of crackers and cheese. "What's the matter, anti-social?" I asked.

Jennifer made a face. "I was raised in the Unitarian faith, or lack of it. Imagine, my parents, perfectly nice Jewish liberals, well assimilated, must needs join together with others of similarly atheistic disposition and try to create rituals for themselves out of thin air. It doesn't work."

Below, women in leather jackets were joining hands with women in pantsuits who were joining hands with women in billowing African print gowns. Candles were lit; the leotarded figure was intoning something about celebrating our sisters, celebrating ourselves, celebrating the publication of a book which represented–

"One woman's accession to tokenhood!" Jennifer burst out rudely. But the celebrants did not hear her.

"Look, do you want to smoke a joint?" Jennifer took it out of the pocket of her vest. It was very plump for a joint, cigar-shaped. "Really good stuff, Panamanian," she said, and I was drunk enough to say yes.

We smoked the whole thing, then slumped down and watched the remainder of the "ritual" in an uncritical stupor.

We didn't move when they turned on the lights. Someone put dance music on the stereo, old Aretha Franklin, and the young and frivolous danced to "Chain of Fools" while the older, wiser heads with serious business to transact retreated to the other end of the loft. There they no doubt proceeded to carve up entire feminist publishing empires, or devised clever strategies for holding the fort against marauding critics from the *New York Review of Books.*

I was regressing rapidly. Leaning my head back, I found I was stoned enough to achieve a sort of neural orgasm, like getting dizzy on a swing. I was remembering what I had once found attractive in (alphabetically): acid, Bob Dylan, easeful death, the Kerouackean ideal, men, Nadine, and all the other pernicious institutions of my ignorant youth, of the time before time began to alarm me, of the epoch before I knew anything at all. We lay on the bed, I remembered. It was winter. Cold afternoon sunlight, Janis Joplin on the FM radio, Nadine's tired, vulnerable face. She said, "My hair smells like you. . . "

I realized that this was all disgusting, and it was late, and Jennifer had left, and I couldn't quite remember whether I'd said goodbye to her. I loathed the prospect of the rain, the IRT. But what I dreaded most was the inevitable insincere farewell scene with Nadine.

And so in the end I did nothing at all until it was too late. Nadine found me there, sat beside me on the mattress, her hand resting on my shoulder. I enjoyed the rise and fall of her voice, the cadence like a stream murmuring over slippery stones, but I couldn't quite avoid hearing the words. It was late, she said; she was tired, she said; depressed, suddenly. What was it all for, after all, she said, the hustling, the compromises, the notoriety. I had always been important to her, she said. My writing. . . my integrity. . . she hoped I knew, didn't think, when we quarrelled that last, worst time, that she meant. . . .

In short, she flirted. I knew it; I allowed it. For maybe fifteen minutes I lay there and she stroked my hair and I felt unrealistic, purely reflexive anticipation tingling in remote corners of my body. At the same time, I was thinking fast.

It occurred to me that my impulse in coming here had been essentially destructive. I had chosen to sacrifice the myth of Nadine Grossman, hitherto preserved at all costs. I had chosen the recognition that time is irrevocable, that we had each changed into different people, that I was no longer the proper instrument for apprehending her.

"I suppose I'd better go home," I said, a bit too tentatively.

"Are you sure you want to? We could go somewhere. I'm still into talking, if you are."

"Talking," that euphemism, irritated me.

"No," I said. "I promised the sitter I wouldn't be late."

"Ah, the ancient problem." She smiled for me the most winning of all her smiles. "Would you like me to come back to Brooklyn with you? Look, I'm staying in a hotel. It wouldn't matter. I'd love to see—Erika, is it?"

"Better not," I said quite firmly; for even at the tender age of thirty I have learned to avoid mornings after. And then, remembering how Nadine had despised what she called my "academic tendencies," I flung Kate Croy's, "We shall never be again as we were," lightly at her and went to get my coat.

Thesis:Antithesis

But we have different voices, even in sleep,
and our bodies, so alike, are yet so different,
and the past echoing through our bloodstreams
is freighted with different language, different meanings—
though in any chronicle of the world we share
it could be written with new meaning
we were two lovers of one gender,
we were two women of one generation.

—Adrienne Rich, *Twenty-one Love Poems*

for Jean

Two women were friends; then they quarreled over politics. But, though the period of their silence and anger with each other lengthened until soon it had been going on for considerably longer than that of their original friendship, oddly enough they did not grow farther apart, did not gradually become indifferent to one another. In the normal course of things they would have realized, on one of their chance meetings (for years they continued to live in the same half-decaying, half-renovated urban neighborhood, moving often but usually ending up within several blocks of each other), that they no longer cared enough to maintain their feud. Then they would have gone out for a cup of coffee, smiled for an hour at memories of youthful folly, and parted amicably with hearty admonitions to "keep in touch." Instead, each found that the momentary encounter, the other's closed face glimpsed in a crowd, continued to inflict acute pain. They avoided one another.

But I have begun badly. In making it appear that I'm competent to give you both women's perspectives on what happened (even that, in a sense, they shared a perspective) I misrepresent my position. In fact, their almost desperate need to understand one another should not be confused with a similarity of outlook. They were so unalike in their approaches to their common experience—and I am so deeply involved in the issues with which they were grappling—that it is probably beyond me to understand them equally or to present them objectively.

Take, for example, my first sentence: "Two women were friends; then they quarreled over politics." Neither Jean nor Amanda would have used the word "quarrel." Amanda would have said that her friend Jean had simply become impossible; that she, Amanda, had had to draw the line somewhere. Or this is how half of her, the rational, injured half, would have explained it. The guilt-ridden, remorseful half would have retorted sarcastically, "Yes, she got to be too much trouble, so you ditched her. You didn't want to be bothered." To be fair, most of Amanda's friends would have corroborated the first explanation; they too found Jean, or rather her politics (but it became increasingly difficult to separate Jean from her politics; this was part of the problem), insufferable.

Jean's view, corroborated by *her* friends, was closer to the second explanation: she had been ditched. After all, Amanda was the one who had come out with, "I don't think we have anything productive to say to each other right now." Jean had made it plain that she wanted to continue their dialogue. For, as she had carefully pointed out, honest and productive relationships are impossible without struggle; isn't that part of the meaning of dialectics? It was unfortunate that Amanda had felt so threatened by Jean's politics, or rather by the politics of her Organization, since their current line had been forged in struggle with other groups on the Left, represented the culmination of a difficult process of learning to take leadership from the proper quarters, and was proven correct on the most basic level by a host of national and international developments. Not that Jean was surprised; she had lost other friends lately. But none of them had been so close to her as Amanda, either politically or (she hesitated slightly before using the word) "personally."

I am assuming, by the way, that we all share a basic, intuitive understanding of the difference between the "political" and the "personal"; despite the feminist proverb which equates the two, I think you will find that, in this story at least, they are hardly interchangeable. It may simply be noted that whereas, in the women's movement in general, the blurring of distinctions between the personal and the political often signals a desire to dismiss the strictly "political," for Jean it was an assertion of the irrelevance of the purely "personal."

In summary, then, while Amanda, in her self-critical moments, faulted herself for having abandoned a *friend*, a "personal" responsibility, Jean emphasized Amanda's evasion of "political" responsibility. But Amanda also had her moments of wondering whether she had not been guilty of political cowardice: perhaps she ought to have been strong enough to continue to subject her every opinion and motive to the grim, battering scrutiny which Jean called "struggle." And Jean, I suppose, felt abandoned and wronged on a personal as well as on a political level, but she tried to set such feelings aside since they were insignificant compared to the much more serious fact of Amanda's political intransigence.

I say "I suppose" because I don't know for sure; of the two, Jean is the one I find much more difficult to understand. The thing is, though, that I try, and in that sense I am, it seems, like Amanda, like Jean; from the beginning their friendship had been based on "understanding," on long conversations in which they sorted out their psychological, aesthetic and political perceptions and values, each attempting to come to terms with the other's point of view.

Their divergent personalities cannot very well be explained by their backgrounds, which appear nearly identical. Their ancestors had immigrated from the same two or three Western European countries in the same decade of the nineteenth century. Both were born, in one of the bleakest years of the Cold War, into white, middle-class, Christian families by whom the Cold War years were not perceived as particularly bleak. They were raised in the suburbs by women who saw motherhood as a profession, and claimed to desire no other. From the first grade on they were tracked into the "gifted" classes. After high school came college; there were no alternatives. The backdrop to higher education was the Viet Nam War which gradually attracted their attention, pointing up the irrelevance of everything they were supposed to be doing. They demonstrated, dropped out, hung out, bummed around, went back, dropped out again, collected food stamps, took money from their parents, stopped taking money from their parents, worked in factories and fast food joints and offices, fled to the inner city. They became "artists," first tentatively, then with increasing dedication, but they never stopped attending political meetings. They learned to identify themselves as feminists, then lesbians. Both were socialists, a term they avoided using because they felt it had become so vague as to be almost meaningless.

We are the same person, Amanda said to herself occasionally, liking the sound of it, not at all sure what she meant. Yet from the beginning they had focused on their differences. Were these really so great, or did they simply loom larger than differences in less important relationships? "Thesis and antithesis," Amanda had once dubbed them, at a point when it was still possible to make such jokes.

"But which of us is which?" Jean had asked. And she had swung into one of her clowning imitations of Broadway routines:

You say po-tay-toes
And I say po-tah-toes
You say to-may-toes
And I say to-mah-toes

Amanda was compulsively punctual, Jean chronically tardy; Amanda was a writer who claimed incomprehension of all other branches of the arts, Jean a painter who wrote poetry; Amanda was the oldest daughter in a prim Protestant grouping of three, while Jean fell somewhere in the middle of one of those sprawling Catholic families of five or six or seven; Amanda was serially monogamous out of habit and preference, while Jean held high the standard of experimental nonmonogamy. And though they appeared for a time to share a comparable level of political confusion, Jean one day ushered in a new era with the ominous remark, "You can't remain unaligned forever. I'm joining a study group."

Of course you are curious about the precise content of the political disagreement which ensued. I have, however, decided against going into all the gory, sectarian details. For one thing, Jean's Organization changed its analysis several times, and to follow this development would be extremely tedious. For another, it was precisely Amanda's problem that she could never care really deeply about the particulars of a given "line"; her clash with Jean was not, in essence, one of belief versus belief, but of belief versus skepticism.

Still, it may prove instructive to trace the form of a policy shift which took place several months after Jean's formal reception into the Organization (an event she jokingly referred to as "taking the veil"). This development, which at first cheered Amanda because it seemed to belie the Organization's reputation for rigidity and dogmatism, later alarmed her. The salutary spring cleaning was, so far as she could tell from Jean's reports, turning into a bit of a purge. They had all, Jean revealed, been opportunist and worse. It now appeared that most of the Organization's work to date had been completely worthless, if not downright counterproductive. Only a thorough renovation of their analysis, a radical overhaul of their methods, a ruthless elimination of members who remained entrenched in the old positions, would enable them to move forward.

Heads rolled, but—somewhat to Amanda's surprise—the Organization pulled through, and Jean with it. True, there were now only about thirty members locally, in addition to a handful of smaller affiliate groups scattered around the Eastern seaboard. But they all had so much energy! And instead of the "lowest common denominator politics" in which (as they now said) they had previously indulged, they began "upping the ante," confronting other groups and individuals on the Left with their new, quite drastic view of what was to be done.

Amanda was now singled out as eminently organizable. She was smiled upon at demonstrations and court appearances, invited to dinners, benefits and forums. She went on one dismal country retreat, sitting around a smoking fire all weekend with some other fellow-traveler types while two or three of Jean's "comrades" (they really used this expression) led discussions of such questions as: How can the lesbian community play a progressive role on the Left? Is it possible to give up privilege? and (thank god for this old standby, which has whiled away many a tedious winter evening), What is the primary contradiction?

Amanda argued, expressed her point of view, but later she was to realize that she had been careful to do this in a way that would be acceptable to the discussion leaders. For example, she questioned the evidence for considering this group more oppressed than that, but she did not question the necessity for devoting so much energy to the ranking of oppressions. She was left with an uneasy sense of having allowed terms to be dictated. She resolved to avoid such predicaments; from now on she would discuss Jean's politics only in one-to-one situations with Jean.

It did not occur to her that she and Jean might stop discussing politics. For what, then, would they talk about? Amanda could see for herself that Jean had less and less of a "personal" life.

Jean reminded Amanda of a woman who claims she's getting married merely in order to furnish her apartment with the wedding presents, then becomes hopelessly enmeshed in her wifely role. Gone were the reservations and questions of which Jean had spoken at the time she "took the veil" (an expression she did not use any more). There was no criticism of her Organization for which she did not have an instant rebuttal, whether in the form of a defense or a shouldering of blame which somehow served to encompass and neutralize the criticism.

Amanda made an effort to recall her old friend Jean: demonstrating fifties dance styles in bars; painting in the morning, paint all over her tennis shoes, light streaming in through the dusty windows of the loft she had long since left for a collective house; waiting out a heat wave in nothing but her ragged underpants, a beer in her hand; telling funny horror stories about her Catholic education. That was the real Jean, not this chain-smoking politico who saw "agents" everywhere and refused to discuss anything on the phone; who spent her days silk-screening posters and her nights attending meetings; and for whom the shit was, always, "finally hitting the fan," the contradictions "heightening" or "intensifying." This new Jean talked too fast.

"Does Jean take speed?" someone asked quite seriously one day.

"No, she's just high on History," Amanda replied cynically.

Their encounters now took on an unvarying pattern. Jean would describe her political activities, interlarding the account with generous doses of political theory. Amanda would respond with questions, criticisms or agreement. Amanda was at this time becoming "more political," which is to say that she more often knew what she thought, began to break out of her old habit of wallowing in helpless admiration of lives she considered more radical than her own. Now that she allowed herself to investigate her opinion of Jean's Organization, she realized that she had simultaneously nurtured two contradictory views of it: that it was a collection of heroically dedicated, morally superior individuals (this, though she of course knew with what withering contempt "morality" is regarded on the Left); that it was a gang of fanatics wearing blinders and driven by complicated needs including deeply painful guilt and a lust for power. Perhaps there was something in each of these views, but could she sustain both?

And why did it matter so much? Why couldn't she just dismiss this particular craziness in the same way she would have done had Jean joined up with the Hare Krishnas or Moonies? She knew people with friends who had done such things, and she knew what their response had been. They had cut their losses.

Amanda felt sure that this *struggle* (Jean's word, of course, but she meant it a bit differently) had been going on almost forever, the form identical and only the content shifting with the times. At a period when religion had been impossible to ignore, she, Amanda, would have been the one tormented by doubt, by the example of Jean's belief. (Jean, on the other hand, was clearly the type to have burned for her too-intense, heretical devotion.) During another explicitly political era—the thirties, say—Jean would have joined the CP while Amanda remained the fellow traveler. Or Amanda would have joined briefly, fleeing in dismay at the time of the Nazi-Soviet pact, while Jean only redoubled her dedication. None of this was original. They might have been crude figures counterposed in some dreadful Herman Hesse novel.

Well, she is the Catholic, I the Protestant, Amanda thought. Her liberal parents, for whom "prejudice" was a cardinal sin, had instilled in her the WASP's usual consciousness of superiority to dogma-ridden Catholics. If she closed her eyes she could still see the copy of *American Freedom and Catholic Power* prominently displayed on their bookshelf.

What if she is right? Amanda would think. The question had the dizzy fascination of a view from an open fifteenth-story window. They could not both be right. *Am I saved*? is really what she meant. But, consciously or not, she had already made up her mind. It was only a matter of time before she would precipitate the fatal conversation, come out with the famous words, "I don't think we have anything productive to say to each other right now."

"Speak for yourself," Jean replied when the time came, sullen, unsurprised, lighting another cigarette.

Amanda did not protest. She had assumed for some time now that she would land the role of heavy in this production. She even enjoyed the dramatic moment in which she got up and walked away from Jean's objections. Partly, this was sadistic pleasure: after all the difficulty, there was some satisfaction in having hurt Jean. Partly it was relief: Jean was not omnipotent, then. Within their relationship her power was great, she set the terms. But Amanda had the ultimate power. She could walk away.

Or so she thought; and for a while she enjoyed her vacation from the complications of Jean. Certainly she felt somehow diminished in her range of possibilities; she would never, for instance, be able to call herself a revolutionary. On the other hand, she was beginning to feel better about the issue-oriented political work she was doing. And she had plenty of friends; she did not need Jean. Life was so much simpler now that she had "given Jean up," which was how she came to think of it, as though Jean were some pleasurable vice: cigars, or an expensive country house.

But the thing was that she had not really renounced Jean. Because she remained on the Organization's mailing list, she was able to keep up with its–Jean's–political development by reading through the ten or fifteen points of unity inevitably printed in miniscule type on both sides of the leaflets that flooded her mailbox. And since the Organization was active in the neighborhood, the walls of abandoned buildings and boarded-up storefronts were always plastered with posters–designed, naturally, by Jean–advertising their forums and demonstrations.

Amanda went away in the summer. When she returned her mailbox was full of propaganda, the storefronts covered with fresh posters. She remembered guiltily that Jean never took vacations. Amanda went to a movie she considered frivolous and encountered several of Jean's "comrades" in the lobby. She promptly experienced a ludicrous sense of relief, as though she had received permission to be there.

Amanda's obsession was shared by some of her friends. Small conclaves devoted hours to discussing, criticizing, and complaining about the Organization, which was, everyone agreed, misguided, crazy, divisive, dangerous, and above all irrelevant. Prediction, often disguised as grim humor, was a favorite pastime at these gatherings.

"Not that I might not endorse terrorism under certain circumstances, but if *they* ever use it I'll know there's something wrong with it," Amanda once remarked.

"Won't it be ironic when we all get put in jail for refusing to testify to the grand jury investigating that crew?" someone responded.

All this was pleasurable, the scratching of a chronic itch, but it represented only one aspect of Amanda's ongoing relationship with Jean. Another was the fact that Amanda had begun to search for Jean's characteristics in other women she met. And then there were the dreams.

These dreams were deeply satisfying, some even sexually so, which was odd given that Amanda had never thought herself to be erotically interested in Jean. But the sexual dreams were not more important than the others, the ones in which there was danger, the city toppling all around, an atmosphere of terror straight out of "The Battle of Algiers"; the ones in which Jean, although dressed in contemporary clothing, was undoubtedly a nun, martyr or religious hermit; the ones in which everything seemed quite normal, they were talking about something insignificant, "personal," as they used to do in the old days, except that there was something just below the surface, everything was about to change, some important secret to be revealed. There was even one dream in which Amanda came up behind Jean as she stood in front of an easel, painting; then stepped aside to reveal a great, vibrant design which, Amanda realized upon waking, could only be described as a mandala. She laughed at herself; she did not approve of Jung. But she found herself waiting to dream this dream over again.

In all these dreams, even the sexual ones, Jean was in some way teacher, mentor. There was a hint of sternness, a whiff of reproach, but also the promise of forgiveness, absolution.

All of this might have gone on indefinitely if the Organization, weary of its righteous isolation, had not relaxed its standards somewhat. ("A lower level of unity is acceptable at this stage of the struggle," was, I believe, how they phrased it.) They launched a fresh "outreach campaign" directed at "all progressive elements" in the local women's community. Amanda began to get phone calls sweetly pressuring her to attend this or that demonstration. Smug as Jesus freaks or Right-to-Lifers, Jean's "comrades" twisted her arm. "Wouldn't you feel a lot better if you did what you know is right?" was their basic attitude.

Amanda was vulnerable because she had been Jean's friend. When she finally grasped this elementary fact, she knew what she would have to do, and did it. She became brutal and sarcastic on the telephone, wrote "return to sender" on all mailed communications, refused leaflets thrust in her face at demonstrations which the Organization's members attended not to offer support but to make converts. The result was that she ceased to be considered a "progressive element." They let her alone.

Still, she could not be sure of her freedom unless she were willing truly to divest herself of Jean. In order to accomplish this, she decided to put Jean into a story, a strategy she had, without realizing it, been saving, saying she did not want to be disloyal.

It worked. She stopped having the dreams. She experienced a bitter sense of triumph, as though, after long planning, she had pulled off the perfect crime. But when she saw the magazine in which her story finally appeared, she understood that what she had written was nothing other than a long love letter to Jean, an explanation and self-justification, a plea for understanding and forgiveness.

This story has, it seems to me, at least three possible (and plausible) endings. Please be assured that my decision to offer you your choice among them has nothing to do with the hackneyed tricks of certain "experimental" writers. Rather, as I indicated earlier, I am more involved than I might wish to be with this subject matter, and am therefore incapable of exercising proper authorial control.

In the first ending, Amanda's half-joking prediction of an extremist direction for Jean's Organization is proven correct. After many months of strenuous "outreach" work, mostly unsuccessful, several members initiate a criticism-self-criticism campaign. A scrutiny of past practice reveals errors so serious that the validity of the Organization's existence is once more cast into doubt. At the same time, the country is moving rapidly to the right. It seems that a change of tactics is called for.

One by one, Jean's cohorts drop out of sight. Months go by; then there is a rash of bombings at selected targets throughout the city. The bombs having been timed to go off at night, there are no injuries except for one security guard who is killed instantly. In their note claiming credit for the explosion, the Organization places the blame for this death unequivocally upon the shoulders of the government and the multinational corporations. About a year after the last of the bombings, Jean is apprehended in a large midwestern industrial city.

Of course Amanda works on her defense committee. The positions of real responsibility are reserved for those who are close to Jean politically, but there's plenty of shitwork left for everyone else. Amanda makes a lot of phone calls, posts a lot of leaflets. She is never to know for sure whether Jean was or was not directly involved in either the planning or the execution of the bombings. Not that it matters.

Jean is magnificent. She takes a principled stand, insisting that her defense emphasize the criminality of the government and the illegitimacy of the institutions which had been targeted, rather than focusing on technicalities. Although barred from reading her own prepared statement at the trial, her presence is itself a statement. Her thinness, her pallor, her hair cropped close to remove the remnants of bleach from her year underground, all somehow underline not vulnerability, but strength. She looks like she's *sure*, like she *knows*, Amanda thinks. Like Joan of Arc at the stake. The characterization is admiring, not sarcastic.

The government's case is weak, so Jean ends up doing a few years at a minimum-security facility where repressive tolerance is the order of the day. From breakfast to dinner the inmates are free to wander up and down corridors painted in dingy pastels. There is a "beauty salon" where they spend hours doing each other's hair and nails. They watch a lot of television.

It is like high school, Jean says, when Amanda goes to visit her. "The sisters really want to get it together, but. . . " The problem, Amanda sees, is that there is very little overt brutality around which to organize. And the lack of it has diminished Jean; she looks listless and bloated. Amanda is reminded of descriptions she's read of mental patients subjected to insulin treatments and electro-shock. Well, an indeterminate sentence and the prison diet would do it to anyone. Amanda goes back again and again, knowing Jean doesn't have many visitors now that her case is no longer publicized. But she dreads the visits.

After Jean's release—she is recommended for parole on grounds of good behavior—they avoid a review of their history. Once, though, Jean tells Amanda about her year underground. "You can't imagine it, it was tremendous, like not having a face or something." Amanda is a bit shocked by the eagerness with which her friend describes this obliteration. Jean is, she realizes, talking about the happiest year of her life.

Back among the living, Jean's time is once more entirely taken up with political work, but work that is, so to speak, more ecumenical than formerly. She lends her name out to worthy causes, is invited to speak with the likes of Martin Sostre, Morton Sobell, Angela Y. Davis. This broadening of perspective is, after all, what Amanda had once hoped for. Why, then, has she come to think of Jean as a has-been? The two are cordial, but they do not meet often.

I should perhaps mention that there is a variant of this particular ending in which Jean is killed—murdered, that is, as the leaflets for the protest demonstration quite accurately state—by police who claim she drew a gun while they were attempting to apprehend her. But I tend to agree with Jean's own analysis that such fates, in this society, are typically reserved for those "more oppressed" than she. Typically—but not always.

According to the second ending, things remain fairly stable for a period of some years. Jean continues her political graphics work, her endless round of dreary meetings, ineffectual demonstrations, lethal criticism-self-criticism sessions. (But these harsh adjectives represent Amanda's perspective; probably Jean herself considers this life quite rewarding.) Jean and her friends never do anything drastic enough to incur more than routine FBI harassment, phone taps, and arrests for unruly courtroom behavior and illegal postering. The Organization, though disliked, has become a fixture on the Left, and as such is tolerated. Its vitality is as mysterious as that of some fundamentalist sect which keeps predicting the Final Days and is not the least bit chagrined when they fail to materialize. The contradictions—make no mistake about this—are heightening, deepening, intensifying.

Then one summer Jean is killed in a car accident. Amanda, hearing the news, experiences a confused sort of grief. But she does not hesitate in deciding to attend the funeral. There she learns what happens to daughters of the middle class who ignore the petit bourgeois custom of making provision for one's own demise: their remains are claimed and borne away by relatives who install them safely in suburban graveyards. It is the most dismal finish Amanda can possibly imagine.

One of the "comrades" invites Amanda to a sort of memorial party or wake held in Jean's old collective house. Amanda is surprised to see how neat and pleasant everything is, not Jean's old chaos, the irrelevance of housekeeping in the face of impending revolution. The walls are covered with Jean's graphics. Amanda notices how good they are. Oh, she had always known Jean was good, of course, but it had been hard to cling to that knowledge in the face of Jean's deprecation of her own talent.

It's not quite fair, Amanda thinks. What she means is that Jean gained a certain moral advantage by pretending to renounce art, while in fact she renounced nothing. "Did she ever talk about me?" she wants to ask Jean's housemates, but doesn't dare. She imagines she recognizes something like her own face in a multi-ethnic grouping on one of the posters, but she can't be sure.

In the third and final ending, nothing happens. Both Amanda and Jean go through many personal and political changes, some of which appear ludicrous to outside observers, but all of which are experienced as internally consistent. Yet the hurt of their rupture remains long after the circumstances which produced it have altered. They cannot seem to transcend this.

Amanda tries—once. After a lapse of months or years, she has another one of her dreams about Jean. Taking this as a sign, she obtains Jean's current phone number, calls her up. Could they meet to talk things over?

Jean is cool, but agrees. They choose a neutral spot for the meeting, a women's bar. Jean is typically late. Amanda sits alone, nervous, drinking her beer, while around her couples sway, dancing, or sit at small tables gazing into each other's faces, no doubt absorbed in romantic dilemmas with which Amanda feels an overwhelming lack of sympathy.

Finally Jean arrives, apologizing perfunctorily for her lateness; she was at a meeting. She orders a drink. They talk, review their history. But they are not getting to the real point.

"I loved you, I always loved you," Amanda says suddenly, risking. In the pause that follows this non sequitur, she hears the jukebox parodying her statement.

"I think," Jean says finally, staring into her drink, "that you've always been so goddamned involved with what I represent, something I mean to you about yourself politically or who you think you ought to be or something, that you don't have the slightest fucking idea what you feel about me personally. So let's not discuss it, okay?"

The truth, Amanda thinks, *but not the whole truth.* Yet what choice has she other than to accept it?

Today is the First Day of the Rest of Your Life

I. 6:40 A.M.

Alice wakes alone in darkness.

Alice, whole in the middle of her life, opens her eyes on the first things. Luminescent clockface, great brown hulk of armchair, the colors of the quilt faded in the deep blue bath of scant light from the frosted airshaft window.

I am myself.

Impossible to tell by the quality of light whether it's cloudy out. Even after years. That's a railroad flat for you. But there is this enormous, unshakable satisfaction rooted far back in her skull, as though she had ascended, direct but unhurried, from the deepest levels of sleep. She's been dreaming, then. There, where she was, was sweetest sex, or music. . .

Trying, she almost gets it. Smiles because it's funny. What's-his-name in the loft, stoned on acid, pumping away. And the acid pumping too, tremendous, with that trick of seeming to amplify each heartbeat. The joke is that, not having done any of this in years, she still dreams about it as though it were somehow important. Improves on it, yet, so that she wakes aroused, wet as she would not have been in real life. Was not, certainly, in that underheated loft, drug-terrified, incredibly ignorant.

Still, if you wanted a baby you'd have to try it again. Briefly, of course. Unless you wanted to use the West Coast turkey-baster method of artificial insemination. A friend just back from the Bay Area has explained it: you find a friendly gay man, he jerks off in the bathroom. . . Several California Amazons are said to have knocked themselves up already, proving conclusively that no doctor is required to mediate between woman and sperm. The approach has all the advantages: a minimum of contact, no expense, and best of all no father to cause trouble later on.

"No fathers," Alice has said to herself many times. "Not this time around. I won't stand for it."

The mechanics of conception seem trivial, actually, given all that follows. For starters, the big belly doesn't fit her current self-image. Not to mention what others would think of her. . . in bars?

Well, as if she went to bars that often, anyway.

Beyond the wall, the ebb and flow of TV noise, ancient as oceans. Superimposed, the comfortable quarrelling of children. "I do not." "You do so." Jackie dominant, trying out her new camp-learned routines, softening her accent, pure white ethnic Brooklyn, to a rather clumsy imitation Black when she says, "Girl, I told you—" "Slap me five." Until finally she is met with the deserved put-down, her friend Delores' dignified, "Why you talkin' to me like that, silly?"

What Alice wants right now is a cigarette and a slow cup of coffee, here, in the dark quiet neatness of her own room. Whole, herself, in this first, best space before everything begins. Not to go out there and face them, children, their cheerfulness, their questions. But in order to reach the kitchen she must pass Jackie's room.

Of course she could simply say good morning, come back with her cup of coffee and shut the door. Jackie and Delores are big now; they would leave her alone for hours. They would probably prefer to get their own sugary breakfast of hot chocolate and Frosted Flakes to eat in front of the TV set anyway. But it's no good; by then it would be too late already for what Alice wants, which is simply unconditional freedom.

What freedom means to me, she thinks, framing it like a composition topic. *Not having to speak to anyone when I get up.*

Babies are different, of course. In return for their gratifying helplessness, you become unselfish, able to accomplish much. Cast as god, you manage to live up to the part. You even get so you enjoy it. Or at least that is what Alice remembers. It's not till later, when they start talking, that you begin to feel like a servant.

If I really had the choice, would I live alone? It's not that she didn't miss Jackie all of August. People form attachments, don't they, and doesn't a woman invariably miss a dead husband whether or not he beat her, whether or not he took out the garbage or brought home the bacon? With Jackie away, a piece of the scenery was missing. But now Jackie has returned, bringing problems, uncertainties, questions that involve split-second decision-making, demands that must be either acceded to or rejected. Worse, she has returned with a large collection of anti-Semitic jokes which she trots out daily over Alice's vehement prohibition. Alice, seeing that Jackie is a failed human being, and unable to escape the logical conclusion that she herself is a failed parent, has difficulty tempering her outrage with reasoned arguments about the causes of the Holocaust.

The disaster occurred in this way: Alice's mother, safe in Minnesota, wrote that she would pay for Jackie to go to a camp of Alice's choosing. Alice, thoughtless, sent Jackie to a camp ("liberal in the worst sense of the word," as she now explains) populated primarily by the children of Jewish professionals. Jackie, however, spent most of her time with a small group of what the camp's brochure solicitously termed "inner city children on scholarship." ("All the Christian kids stuck together, Mom," Jackie reports. "We had to," while horrified Alice attempts to establish that Jackie's no "Christian kid.") In plain language, Jackie hung out with an angry, virtually ostracized minority of Black children, learning to dance elegantly to disco tunes, interject "slap me five" at appropriate intervals, and tell anti-Semitic jokes. Indeed, so clearly and fiercely were lines drawn and sides taken at this dreadful camp that Jackie has been unable to interpret Alice's remonstrances as anything but an attack on her Black friends. Meanwhile, she rejects any suggestion that she must have had a difficult month at camp, and "Jew" has become her favorite epithet.

Nothing for it but to begin, then. Alice rises, throwing off the sheet, the quilt it's finally September and cool enough for. The full-length mirror draws her, though she despises it, plans to get rid of it, would never have it if it hadn't been there already when, years ago, she moved in. There she stands, naked in her white skin, her sturdy body a souvenir of unimaginable female ancestors who spent their lives in darkest Western Europe bearing children and cultivating potatoes. She turns for the side view, sucks her stomach tight, then lets it slack for a dose of realism. Alice believes in facts, and facing them. Things, irrevocable things, have happened since she was twenty. Jackie turned her belly button inside out, popped it to convexity in the eighth month.

She wonders what the one from the bar, the kid, the Catholic, Theresa, saw; was it this Alice of the solemn face, eye-wrinkles, chin-acne, or someone else? When you are young, she thinks—well, younger, no need for melodrama now—you don't understand how your youth covers everything. The fat on Theresa's bones was young fat, that made it different.

She steps into her slippers, reaches for the pack of Marlboros, watching herself remembers she's trying to quit. *And why Marlboros, still, after all these years?* Is it because of the ads? Really, she'd like to be the Marlboro man, riding that horse alone under the great sky. More probably it has to do with the fact that out of the three men she's fucked in her life—not counting Jackie's father, of course; Jackie's father one didn't fuck—two smoked Marlboros. The third, the one in the loft with the acid, smoked Pall Mall nonfilters, out of the question in these enlightened times. *I spent all those years trying to keep up with the boys.* The cigarette dangles toughly from her lip; oh, she would look smashing in bars! If only she knew how to play pool. . . .

Alice slips on her robe, pads down the hall to the bathroom. She turns on the light to scare away the roaches, breathes through her mouth to ward off the sweet, amoniac stench of the catbox. *I ought to dump that litter right away,* she thinks;

then doesn't. Jackie's door is firmly shut, giving her a good view of the dreadful poster that has graced it for six months now. "Today Is The First Day Of The Rest Of Your Life," it alleges in Olde English characters.

"But Mom, it's mine, I like it," Jackie says each time Alice complains.

"Right on, but do I have to look at it every time I walk down the hall?" Alice answers.

"I have to look at all your posters," Jackie replies sweetly, stopping Alice cold. Alice firmly expects a new stage and more posters, hazy photographs of straight couples making out on sunset beaches, slogans from Fritz Perls and Erich Segal. But she keeps quiet about it.

Now, smoking fast, she lights the burner under the kettle. She prefers not to smoke in front of Jackie, who knows she is trying to quit and makes an issue of it. Which would not be so terrible if it meant that Jackie herself would never smoke, but Alice knows it will mean nothing of the sort in five years when Jackie's fourteen and hanging out on street corners (everything is accelerated now, of course; Jackie at fourteen will be Alice at twenty-two). Then Jackie will smoke if she damn well pleases, and come up with the necessary justifications. For some reason Alice flashes on the therapist sitting there in her sunny, ordered, plant-green office, saying, "But Alice, do you *like* your daughter?" For a week or two she had thought it important to address this question seriously. Then she had realized she was not, in fact, all that fond of the therapist, and had stopped seeing her.

The truth is that Alice *likes* Delores, for example, much more frankly and simply than she likes Jackie. One invests too much in one's own flesh and blood. In a better society, of course, children will be raised collectively and parents will not regard them as investments, a term clearly derived from the capitalist economic model of human interaction, but meanwhile—

A heavy tread in the hall; Alice steels herself.

"Fee, fi, fo, fum, hey Mom, you smoking again?" Jackie, predictably, is hanging out of her pajamas, buttons missing, holes at elbows and knees. She looks to have gained a few pounds at camp; her face is brown, her nose peeling and her sandy hair—oh, almost-blonde, the miracle of it in New York City, how the old ladies used to stop Alice in the Stuyvesant Town days to cluck over the Aryan darling in a stroller—has bleached out several shades. Delores is as thin as ever, bundled primly into her blue rayon robe, her hair in tight pigtails, one big pink curler in front.

"Well, and a very good morning to you, too," Alice can't resist retorting nastily, in the manner of those obnoxious grownups from her own past—her mother was one—who would shame a child forgetful of "thank you's" with a premature "you're welcome."

It doesn't work. "Mom, I thought you were trying to quit," Jackie persists.

"I'm cutting down, Jackie, okay? Don't hassle me about it. What do you and Delores want for breakfast?"

"How should I know? I'm not hungry yet."

"Well, I'm serving pretty soon, so you'd better hurry up and get hungry."

"All right." But it is the long-suffering, plaintive "all right" which will be heard with increasing frequency as the dark night of adolescence approaches. "Eggs?"

"Since when do you eat eggs?"

"What do you mean, I eat eggs."

"You didn't last time we discussed it. Did you learn to eat them at camp?"

"Mom, I said I eat eggs." That warning note in her voice: don't mess with me.

"All right, all right. Go take your shower and I'll have them ready when you come out. What about you, Delores?"

"I'm not hungry, thanks."

Delores' eating habits are far worse than Jackie's. Delores' idea of breakfast—or lunch, for that matter—is a half a package of Malomars and a carton of orange drink. Still, unreasonably, Alice is far more irked by Jackie's sugar consumption.

"Oh come on, Delores," she now cajoles dutifully. "Have you forgotten we eat breakfast in this house? Eggs for you, too?" And then, seeing it won't work, offers up her bargaining chip: "How about Frosted Flakes, then?"

Of course, the variable which goes uncontrolled-for in Alice's most serious analyses of her own attitude toward the children is the fact that Delores is Black. Certainly this circumstance enters into the equation, though by now Alice has begun to recognize a certain futility in her efforts to figure out just how. Yes, she is insufferably, liberally delighted that her daughter's best friend is Black, and what should she do about it? Is she somehow responsible? She thinks not. She was, it seems to her, careful to encourage this friendship no more nor less than any other. And look at the outcome: Jackie is so happy to be reunited with Delores that she has gone off quite cheerfully to her shower, where she can be heard singing at the top of her lungs: "At McDonald's, at McDonald's, we do it all for you-hoo-hoo."

As for Delores' own feelings, Alice is never quite sure. Clearly she likes Jackie. Clearly, also, she relishes the spaciousness, the relative freedom of a home uncluttered with smaller children. But does Delores like her, Alice, personally?

Sometimes Alice thinks she detects a secret current of understanding between them, and feels guilty. Alice and Jackie are the couple, after all; what right have Alice and Delores to particular friendship? On the other hand, there were times they met on the street during Jackie's month at camp when Alice was quite sure Delores wouldn't have spoken if she hadn't said hello first. Was that because Alice is a grownup, or was it that, living on the same block, even, they live in separate worlds? For Jackie and Delores, being small and as yet half-formed, have a certain flexibility, mobility, whereas she, Alice, is fixed in her privileged place. *Like those shellfish, adrift in youth, that attach themselves to a rock and stay put for the rest of their lives.* Alice has been in Delores' mother's apartment—no bigger than her own, home to five children—only twice.

"So what have you been doing this past month, Delores?"

"Reading, mostly. The library had a contest."

"And did you win?" Alice sets the plates of eggs down on the table along with the box of Frosted Flakes for Delores, filters herself a cup of coffee.

"No, it wasn't that kind of contest," Delores says, patient with the hopelessly conservative outlook of middle age. "Winning isn't important. It was a contest with yourself."

Nothing is so dismal as eating breakfast with children, Alice thinks, though Delores and Jackie are in such a good mood that they eat quickly, without complaints. *If I were free, I would have gone out to breakfast on a morning like this. A wonderful fall morning, blue and unhumid, though the leaves haven't really started turning yet. I would have had home-fries, the New York Times crisp and fresh beside the plate.* Then she remembers her ex-friend Morgan the anti-imperialist saying, "You have to read the *Times* to see how the State is moving, what it wants the white middle class to think," and feels ashamed of her enthusiasm for that reactionary organ. *Full of lies,* she reminds herself sternly. *Little white lies,* she thinks, hearing the phrase reverberate in all its irony.

The children have disappeared; Alice finishes her coffee and, musing on the politics of language, gets up to spray her plants. Today is the day she is finally going to Do Something About Her Roach Problem.

II. 10 A.M.

In the women's bathroom at the unemployment office a young mother is exercising her inalienable right to mortify her child's flesh. Alice, standing in a puddle of water from an overflowed sink, her hands under the blow dryer, grasps the whole situation the minute she notices the effort at composure that distorts the woman's face, the way she jerks her little boy by the elbow. "There," she pants, breathless with fury, "now you'll get what I told you. Now I'll give you something to cry about." And she actually lifts up the light jacket to secure a better target.

The thing is that the boy, who is perhaps three and a half, is not crying, and he does not cower beneath the impact of the broad, strong, ring-laden hand. In fact, he betrays neither apprehension nor interest in the proceedings. He simply stares at the floor, the wall, *waiting for it to be over,* Alice thinks, *like a prostitute in bed with a john.*

She perceives she should do something; perceives, at the same time, there's nothing to be done. Recently she read an article on preventing child abuse which suggested that bystanders offer assistance to harassed parents. But "Excuse me, you've got your hands full there, want me to hold him while you hit him?" hardly seems a constructive opener. *When he's twelve he'll be mugging old ladies in tenement hallways.*

The blow dryer is ludicrously inefficient. Alice wipes her hands on her jeans and goes out to stand in one of the lines (*on line,* a real New Yorker would say). Too late, she realizes the line she picked isn't moving at all; up front an old man is trying to argue with the clerk in a language that is neither English nor Spanish. She ought to have brought a newspaper.

After a while she spots the young mother standing in line too, her pretty face emptied now of anger and every other emotion, so perfectly tensionless she might almost be high on smack or watching television. Whatever can she be thinking? Evidently she is not thinking of her son, who, evidently not thinking of her, plays on the dirty tile a few steps away. Probably she is not thinking of anything; probably she is just tired.

Alice wishes they could talk. She would ask friendly questions: *Haven't you observed the addictive effect of these beatings, don't you find you need more and more to achieve an equivalent response? Do you realize it can only become worse as he gets older?* But the mother would misunderstand, would certainly react with defensive indignation. For aren't mothers, with all their dreadful burden of responsibility, entitled to some privileges? Is it not accepted the world over that women will be exempt from criticism when they quietly haul their children into restrooms and beat the shit out of them? Alice wonders what the kid did, anyway. Probably nothing much. So many minor transgressions can seem intolerable at the time.

Alice swore off her own relatively modest program of corporal punishment when she realized the tactic neither diminished her own anger nor impressed Jackie with her authority. Later, however, she was plagued by a recurring dream in which she would hit Jackie over and over in horrible slow motion, the frustration mounting with each blow. In those dreams Jackie always looked as the little boy had: impassive, never frightened, never sorry.

Does the woman who dreams thus of the child that exists already have the right to consider having another?

The problem of physical punishment is of course part of the much larger problem of parental authority in general. Alice, an expert at challenging several types of authority, does not have much confidence in any, which can be disastrous; believers always make the best miracle-workers. And there are still believers and miracles; quiet Mrs. Perez in the downstairs apartment, for example, has three well-scrubbed, impeccably-behaved children under the age of six. Alice is still ashamed to encounter her in the hall because, in the days when Jackie had frequent tantrums, she would open the window of her room and holler down the airshaft, "My mother is a whore, my mother is a turd, my mother is a cocksucker."

By the time she reaches the front of the line sheer boredom has obliterated Alice's nervousness at signing for her first check. And then everything goes smoothly; both the clerk's obvious alienation and the fact that she is clearly not intended to read the fine print at the bottom of the IBM card belie the prominently posted signs which caution against misrepresentation in applying for benefits. The carefully-faked list of job interviews is not required. Still, she leaves the office quickly, feeling just a little too lucky. For her unemployed status is "arranged." And with all her experience, the food stamps, even AFDC once, the successful shoplifting sprees from her married days (Peter never could understand how she managed steak so often on their budget), she's still waiting to get caught every time she looks to get what her mother would call "something for nothing."

Once out on Flatbush, though, in the strong, cool sunshine, the renewed atmosphere of fall, she feels elated. *Not to be in the office on a weekday morning. To walk somewhere instead of taking the train.* Being out on the street when others have to work has always given her a delicious little illusion of superiority, of getting something extra, as staying up late used to do when she was little. Really, if it weren't for Jackie, she thinks she'd rather work odd hours, rotating shifts, weekends, anything but a straight nine-to-five. She takes in the impossibly young women pushing strollers, dragging their older children along on the grim errand of shopping for school supplies, and thinks *yes it's going to be winter and the heat will break and Jackie will get sick every other week and so what. I'm going to be all right now, I really am. I'm going to have time. Maybe even start running in the park again, join another study group or something.*

Alice stops to buy a gallon of cockroach poison and a plastic spray container, then lugs them up the hill past Lawyer Abogado; past Psychic Reader Leerte La Suerte ("We Solve All Problems Of Live"); past Cafe Borinquen and Karate College; Comidas Criollas y Chinas; the Blarney Stone Bar; the Holy Spirit Temple; Iglesia Pentecostal; The Charismatic Revival Center; past the Palace Theatre where "Dorothy's Desire" plays on a double bill with "The Cunning Linguist"; past Mayaguez Grocery and Chinese Takeout and Junque Antiques and Shabbazz Products; past La Botanique de St. Jacques Majeur with its window display of dusty white Virgins, dusty brown Virgins, and even—she stops in passing to marvel at it—one dusty brown Virgin holding a dusty, anemic-looking white Jesus.

"What took you so long, Mom?" Jackie and Delores are draped listlessly on the stoop, the picture of pre-adolescent decadence.

"Did you want me for something?"

"No, I just don't like when you go for so long. What if somebody bothers us?"

"You've got your key; you could have gone inside." But Alice registers a twinge of guilt; what, in fact, if someone had bothered them?

"Inside is boring."

"I'm sorry if it seemed long. I had to stand in line, and then I walked home."

"Couldn't you take the bus?"

"Sure, but what for?"

"It's quicker."

"Yes, and someday my legs would atrophy and fall off. Do you kids want to come upstairs with me?" But really she doesn't want them to; Jackie's refusal is a relief even though it means the two of them are probably plotting to sneak around the corner for pizza. What does Alice care? She is going to clean her apartment.

When Alice lived with Leah, Leah had branded her "compulsive." And it must be admitted that, like her mother before her, Alice cannot refrain from bending down to pick up a thread or scrap of paper or piece of lint from a recently-vacuumed, if stained and threadbare, carpet. The truth, however, is really a bit more complex. Alice dreads cleaning as much as she looks forward to it.

What really upsets her is not the work itself, but its repetitive character. As a child she was exhausted by the very idea of the body's functioning, the realization that the lungs are never able to rest from their labor of breathing in and out, the heart to be still, not even in sleep. Now she is exhausted by the thought that always, for the rest of her life, she will have to do her own housework. Nothing can release her from this prospect, not even money, if she had it, which she won't; for Alice believes firmly that people ought to clean up their own shit. Yet if envious bad feeling could kill, Jackie's father Peter's current wife, a petite blonde who sells real estate, would keel over like a poisoned cockroach in the spotless kitchen of her St. Paul split level, for she has a woman in twice a week to clean.

The second disturbing thing about cleaning is that it forces Alice to take a close look at her apartment. And when she does so every water stain on the ceiling, every bit of crumbling plaster, every grease spot on the kitchen wall pains her unutterably, as though she had expected more of a decrepit railroad apartment in a shoddy eight-family building too far away from the park to have been solidly constructed in the first place. There is a part of Alice that clearly ought to live in the suburbs, in one of those houses her mother aspired to, where everything works because nothing is more than a year or two old. As it is, she has always before her the reproachful image of her mother's small, square, ugly brick bungalow where the floors are mopped twice a week, where the shelves of the linen closet are labelled "double sheet, bottom," "single sheet, bottom," "pillowcases"; where someone—her father, during his lifetime, and now some neighborhood handyman—is called in immediately to replace a broken tile, paint a stained wall, fix a leaky faucet.

So Alice hates cleaning. And yet Alice loves cleaning because of its wonderful internal logic, which relieves her of responsibility. Objects dictate, for a change; the room involves her, takes her out of herself. Her thoughts float free on the surface and order themselves along with the furniture, books, plants, dishes, spice jars, cannisters of beans and dried peas, drawersful of clothing.

For a long time Alice has been thinking about cleaning without actually cleaning. Now the refrigerator disgusts and depresses her with its scabrous bits of food in old yogurt containers, its limp scallions and wilted lettuce leaves steeping in greenish liquid at the bottom of the vegetable bin. But she handles it; is, in fact, amazed at her own energy as she hurls rotten food into the garbage, sponges down the porcelain with baking soda. The sounds of the late sixties accompany her, blasting from an FM station that specializes in hard-rock nostalgia.

Alice, even with years and years of piano lessons behind her, doesn't give a fig for music; it is the mood certain music creates that she responds to. For instance, there's that old Buffalo Springfield song, circa 1967, maybe even earlier: "Stop, hey, what's that sound. . . . " And as though the appropriate cluster of brain cells had been electronically stimulated, it conjures up a precise memory of a spring day, humidity, a certain street in the East Village already beginning to smell of garbage. It is evening; Alice, bathed in a slowly receding acid glow, walks the street in her young body past tulip trees and a few runty daffodils. The drug has left her ego there intact like something fascinating washed up on the beach; after her short vacation from her personality she is pleased with herself. It is anticipation she is full of, though she is only going home, after a day spent in clumsy, drug-saturated adultery, to boring Peter in boring Stuyvesant Town, who will be angry in response to her diffidence, who will thunder his famous threat: "I don't think New York is doing you any good. I'm going to request a transfer back to St. Paul."

The first rule of social organization in New York City is that phones not taken off the hook inevitably ring; therefore it is unreasonable of Alice to be irritated when hers does, just as she's feeling good seeing the room begin to smooth into order, just as she's humming and filling the mop pail. Dutifully she answers, really not wanting to talk to anyone but motivated by the typical New York fear of missing something.

It is Morgan the principled, to whom, theoretically, she no longer speaks. There is a trial; there is to be a demo.

"Oh shit Morgan, I forgot. New Jersey. What a hassle. I really want to go, but I've got to think what to do with Jackie." No, no, she doesn't want to go, dreads the long car trip pressed knee to knee with strangers, the boredom of waiting to get into the courtroom, the awkward proximity to Morgan, the patronizing smiles with which the real politicos will greet and dismiss her, bourgeois idealist, mere fellow traveler, liberal.

But a woman, a Black woman, a woman younger than Alice and of legendary courage, a woman who has been ill and alone and has refused to betray her convictions or her people, a woman who can perhaps count on the fingers of one hand the times she's seen real sunlight during the past year—this woman is in great danger of being put away for the rest of her life. And it would be wrong not to protest, indecent not to mark the occasion with an appropriate ritual, a show of bodies and voices. Wouldn't you want a memorial service if you were about to be buried alive? Wouldn't you?

Besides, what would happen if Alice, for just one day, did precisely what she wanted? *No one would ever speak to me again, that's what.*

"There's no problem about Jackie," Morgan is assuring her. "Bring her. Helen is bringing Elisha, and I'm sure there'll be other kids." In Morgan's circles, high pressure sales tactics in the service of the revolution are held to be no vice.

Ignore it, maybe it'll go away. "Of course I'll give her the option, but I doubt she'll want to go. Generally she hates demos. And if she doesn't want to be there she'll just make both of us miserable."

"Well, look, I need to know soon about space in the car."

"Can I call you back in a couple hours?" Seldom have a mop pail, an expanse of filthy floor, looked so inviting.

"No later than five. I've got to get this thing set up; there's a defense committee meeting tonight, and I have to run off some leaflets and get them into the city."

"Okay, speak to you soon." *Almost home free.*

"Oh Alice, by the way—"

"Yeah?" *Here comes your nineteenth nervous breakdown.*

"Maybe it wouldn't hurt to struggle with Jackie around that business about the demo." So matter-of-factly she gets it out, with the calm assurance of one who is doing a favor for everybody concerned: Alice, Jackie, radical politics. . . .

Alice, indignant, blows it. "You mean I should try to guilt-trip Jackie into going to the demo?"

"I mean just what I said. We all struggled with Elisha for months before she would go to court around the grand jury business, but now she goes, and she really understands it, too. She even made up a little book with drawings and everything called "What Kids Can Do To Stop Grand Jury Repression."

"Look, Morgan, I know you've got your leaflets to deliver, and I happen to be in the middle of something myself. So probably I shouldn't even get into this, but I have to say I really don't believe in imposing my politics on Jackie. I think in the long run kids just end up resentful. New York is full of children of Communists who've joined the Hare Krishnas or something, or they're just plain awfully fucking middle class."

"What does the C.P. have to do with it? Revisionism—"

It is Alice who ends up resentful, hanging up the phone after the fifteen-minute conversation that ensues. This sort of exchange is exactly what she and Morgan are supposed to be avoiding by avoiding each other. If she had any guts, she thinks, she'd make a clean break, tell Morgan to go to hell, quit calling her up with these goddamned political announcements.

But that isn't all of it. She can't blame Morgan entirely for the depression that inevitably sets in following these conversations. *Oh shit, shit, shit, just when I was feeling fine,* she catches herself thinking. *Why me?* And then, predictable equal and opposite reaction: *Why not? What right in the world do I have to expect to be happy?* Underground, her spirit pressed beneath the building's weight, in terrible New Jersey, sits a woman in danger and pain, a woman more alone than Alice has ever been. Before her looms the behavior modification unit, the so-easily-arranged fatal accident revolutionaries and even simple agitators tend to meet up with in federal prisons.

Calmly, as one recognizes the fatal turning point in the familiar bad dream, Alice notes the onset of the one mood she most dreads: the conviction that she is simply wrong, wrong at every level and in every way, wrong to an extent that is not correctible within the limits of her personality, her circumstances. Not *in the wrong,* but wrong; not *mistaken,* but herself the mistake.

She remembers the feel of her chest, childish-flat under the thin material of her dress, the leap of her heart as she pressed her hand over it standing in that classroom in flat and barren St. Paul in the 1950's, repeating the Pledge of Allegiance but not listening to the words, awed by some emotion that wasn't patriotism, really, was more like the realization of her own marvelous good luck, the sheer statistical improbability that had made her, of all things there are to be, white American. Yet even then inside her elation had been a nervousness.

Now she knows why. The obverse of that elation is the question: *Why am I not someone else? Why not the Palestinian bombed in refugee camps, leukemia-stricken citizen of Hiroshima, Black women, pregnant, strung up on a tree, raped, slit open somewhere in the South, Black man dead of cop-bullets in any of a hundred northern cities? Amass all the weighty credentials of my oppression: lesbian, single mother, unemployed, over thirty, working-class background, no college degree. Put it all together, heap it up, I still can't feel I don't deserve to be dead.*

Survivor-guilt, she whispers, expecting the phrase to do something; but it floats, obstinate, refusing to attach itself to any part of her problem, refusing to help out, then plummets into darkness till the echo rushes back: *liberal guilt, liberal guilt, liberal guilt.* There is no help.

Sick to death of herself, her so-predictable thought processes, Alice drinks a cup of tea. Now she must mop. Later, when she has figured out what to do with Jackie, she will call Morgan and reserve a seat in a car to New Jersey.

Gradually labor soothes her; furniture reasserts its objective influence. Pushing the mop, she sees herself pushing the mop. Alice Paleface, the last WASP in New York, guesses it doesn't matter what she feels.

III. 1:25 P.M.

The kitchen reeks of roach poison. Alice distracts herself from the stench by reading the "Home" section of the *Times* while she eats her lunch: Mimi Sheraton on several outrageously expensive restaurants; a feature on a young "bachelor" (a faggot, clearly, though the *Times* doesn't quite say so) who resides in SoHo in something called a "minimalist loft." His kitchen—a stove, sink and refrigerator along one wall—is handily concealed by a pushbutton-controlled sliding panel; his bathroom is a toilet and tub in a corner, and readers are assured that a portable folding screen is kept handy in a closet (voluminous closets are, apparently, an indispensable feature of a minimalist lifestyle) "for the convenience of my mother, when she visits." Cost of renovations: under sixty thou. Alice gets as far as this eccentric householder's explanation that he is not a materialist before being interrupted by the children.

No, they do not want lunch. Pizza sauce still clings to the corners of Jackie's mouth, and under pressure they admit to having "gone around the corner." No, they will not do so again without asking permission. Yes, they understand that a slice of pizza is an inadequate lunch. Yes, they will eat a piece of fruit later.

They sit there glumly, watching Alice chew. They do not seem to have anything to say. End-of-summer doldrums, Alice diagnoses, and is about to banish them when Jackie bursts into sudden, dramatic tears.

"What's the matter?" Alice is calm, for Jackie's tears are usually sudden and dramatic. Now she is inarticulate with anguish, clasping Alice around the neck, her hair hanging into Alice's plate, each sob an escalation.

Who is it has paid mourners at their funerals? Alice tries to remember. *She ought to hire herself out.* But dares not express any sarcasm, being the mother.

It is Delores who finally has to intervene, explaining, "That Leroy up the block called her a bad name, Alice."

"And what name was that?" Alice asks very, very lightly, because she thinks she knows and so is terrified.

Alice, mind you, belongs to a brave, new, incredibly privileged generation which hardly knows the meaning of the "lesbian oppression" it's always talking about. Alice herself has never suffered the slightest doubt as to whether, despite her sexual orientation, she is in fact a full-fledged human being. Alice is not afraid of anything. It's just that she's always waiting for this disaster to overtake her child, these words to fall from the sky, more bruising and dangerous than any sticks or stones. *Dyke. Bulldagger. Fruit. Which are you, a girl or a boy?*

"I don't like to say it," Delores apologizes. "He called her a white bitch."

Jackie surprises everyone by chipping in, "Yeah, and I didn't do anything, and we were just walking down the block eating our pizza and he starts following us going 'white bitch, white bitch.' " Then she relapses into her desperate keening.

"Oh Jackie," Alice says cheerily, relief flooding her voice, "that was certainly a mean thing to say. Which one is Leroy, is he that big boy who lives in your building, Delores?"

"No, that's Arthur. Leroy's just a little kid, about six years old. But mean, though. He's got a nasty mouth, my mama says."

"Did you hear that, Jackie? If you'd calm down a minute we could talk about this. Delores says Leroy has a nasty mouth. Probably he was just feeling unhappy this morning and you were the first person he ran into." Alice is conscious of a certain hypocrisy in offering this simplistic explanation, but the situation seems too critical for subtleties. Best to keep talking, try to provide some distraction.

"What did you say back to him, anything?"

"I called him a Jew, a fucking stupid Jew."

Count ten; be mature, adult; believe, oh believe, that all trials in time will pass. Express your point of view, but without rancor; don't be judgmental.

But even Alice can hear that the ice of parental disapproval has formed instantaneously on her vocal chords as she says, "Jackie, I don't think that was a good thing to say at all. For a number of different reasons."

"Well, he is, and I'm glad I said it, so there."

"What do you mean? He's not Jewish, he's Black." The wrong tack, certainly, but she can't resist; Jackie's sheer illogic compounds her fury.

"There's Black Jews. You said so once."

"Leroy certainly is not one of them. Anyway, that's hardly the point. The point is, if you don't like being called a white bitch then you ought to be able to figure out what's wrong with using 'Jew' like it was some kind of swearword."

Jackie only looks sullen and conscious of injustice.

"How do you think your Jewish friends would feel if they heard that? Evie and Meredith and Rachel. And Leah; what do you think she'd say?"

At this, a flash of animation from Jackie: "Leah's your friend, not mine."

"All right. But the rest, then."

"Oh Mom, you don't even *care* about what Leroy said to me," and Jackie prepares to burst into tears again.

"No, I do care. But I think there are lots better ways to deal with it."

"What do you want me to do, hit him? I bet I could really waste him, but Carole at karate says we're only supposed to use it for emergencies."

"I'd like to hit him," Delores ventures, uncharacteristically bloodthirsty. "He's got no business talking like that when people are just walking down the street. Anyway, I don't think it was 'cause he just felt mean this morning, like you said. I think it's 'cause he hates white kids."

Ah, the heart of the matter. Alice, caught out in a weak analysis, takes refuge in a question. "And why do you suppose he hates white kids?"

"I don't know. Isn't it stupid? Everybody's just people anyway." Delores tosses this off so coolly that you might think she not only believed it, but knew it to be a commonly accepted fact. Politicians are crooked, the sky is blue, everybody's just people anyway. Oh, she is dishonest: two-faced little snip, crafty native lying, for the best of reasons, for survival, to obtuse European colonialist. Extra, extra, read all about it: Delores has reasons for not trusting her friend Alice.

Alice the exceptional grownup, the good honky, is stung by the reminder, hides it. "It seems to me Leroy probably has some good reasons for feeling angry at white kids."

"Uh-uh," Delores insists. "Nobody hurt him or anything. He was just born mean." *As Morgan would say, an undialectical view of Leroy.*

"Oh, Leroy, Schmeroy." Thus Jackie, miraculously recovered from her grief, her eyes perfectly dry though her cheeks are still blotched red. "I don't even *care* about Leroy. He's just a baby anyway."

"What in the world are we talking about, then?" But Alice, though irritated, recognizes in operation Jackie's amazing knack of finally getting around to the real emotional point (*oh in this I've done well,* she thinks, modestly taking credit, *she's so in touch with her feelings*).

"I just want to know why I have to be the only one that's different, that's all."

Alice is mystified, as perhaps she's meant to be. "Different from what?"

"Just different. From everybody. I mean, everybody's something. Everybody's Black or Italian or Jewish or Puerto Rican or Catholic or Irish or Lutheran or something. I'm the only one who's nothing."

"Oh sweetheart." Alice wants to laugh, and though she doesn't it shows. "You and me both," she says, hugging Jackie. "We're in the same boat, we're both nothing. It's called being a WASP, a plain, boring old American. Some places they're in the majority, though not on this block, not on the IRT express, not in the world."

She is too easily amused. "Not you," and Jackie pulls away. "You're—you know, you're with women." By which Alice understands that her daughter is too prudent to use the word "lesbian" in front of her guest. And perhaps she's right. Though the apartment is full of posters, books, magazines on which that word is emblazoned, and though Delores has been coming over for years without incident, still it is true that some things are best left unarticulated. "It's just me, I'm the only one who's nothing," Jackie concludes, and begins to wail again, impressed by her own presentation.

Melodramatic, but alarming: what if she really feels herself such an outcast? "Jackie, come on now, when we go to St. Paul—"

"I wish we lived in St. Paul!" Jackie flings it down with the defiant conviction of "I wish I were dead!"

"What a gruesome thought. Thank god we don't." Though she hasn't seen a Minnesota winter in twelve years, when Alice imagines life in St. Paul she somehow pictures herself marooned in the middle of a vast shopping mall parking lot in January: the snowdrifts, the early dark, the heavy parcels tearing at her arms, dim hordes of children clutching incongruous skirts, car nowhere in sight. "When I was growing up in St. Paul almost everybody was the same, or it seemed like that to me anyway. It was awfully boring. In a lot of ways you're lucky to live someplace where you meet different kinds of people."

"That's what you think. At Daddy's—" But Jackie stops there; for what is there to be said about Daddy's, where she spends two ritual weeks each year? There is nothing in the least remarkable about Daddy's; it is simply a bland, solid all-American home; that is its charm.

"Would you like to spend more time in St. Paul next summer? You could stay awhile with your grandma. You're big enough to fly out and back by yourself now."

"I don't know. I want to be with you, Mom."

"Well, you could think about it." But expressions of dependency, rare from Jackie, usually win Alice over. And so they embrace, and Jackie climbs into her mother's lap and remains there for a while, like a smaller kid than she is, really.

I'm not so bad at this, I'm really not so bad at this business of being a mother, Alice thinks later, elated, having calmed the children and sent them back outside with an apple apiece and an admonition to ignore Leroy. *I manage; I explain; I guide; we pass through the moments of anger, misunderstanding, on the other side come together. It will be all right. Now that she's begun to talk about it, maybe she'll even get over this anti-Semitic business sooner or later.*

But vacuuming her livingroom rug she puts it all together, sees things differently: how the children protect her, each other, themselves; how she protects herself protecting them. And where have they learned to lie, Delores not wanting to say what she knows about racism, pretending to believe that people are people are people. Jackie unable to lash out at Leroy with the first, obvious weapon ready to hand: *Black bastard.* She wonders if perhaps they really imagine her to be as innocent as she has wanted tò imagine them. Maybe they really think she thinks she lives, they all live, in the better world she has tried to get them to act as though they live in; maybe their guilt is that they cannot share her imagined innocence.

Understanding this, sorting it all out in great rhythmic strokes of the vacuum clearer, Alice comes to pity them, and by extension herself and everyone. She even goes to the window, stands there half-ready to call them back, hold them, while she explains how we must be kind to others and ourselves, people try, nothing is anybody's fault except Rockefeller's or the Chairman of the Board of IBM's, and they are not people anymore, nor animals, but clones, mutants, cancer cells to be eradicated and then we'll finally be free. *El pueblo unido jamás será vencido.* That old, fervent prayer from a thousand demonstrations.

Except that it is not true. A phrase, something Morgan once said, comes back to her, never mind Morgan said it: *In a racist society there are no exceptions.*

Looking down, Alice sees that Jackie and Delores have join joined with five or six other children in one of those mysterious sidewalk games full of violent motion, unknown to her from her childhood of St. Paul backyards, sedate hopscotch and "Mother may I?" and tag. They are completely involved, would look up at her with scorn, would answer even the most reasonable request with sarcasm, sudden child separatists that they are.

She closes the window. How can she plead not guilty? An ineradicable fantasy, a fantasy she has never admitted to anyone, stains her consciousness as visions of the flesh taunted the saints of old: a Black man will rape her, she will get pregnant, will keep the child. It gives her a hideous, tainted pleasure to imagine the curious or disapproving glances cast in her direction as she walks down the street pushing the stroller with the little dark child in it, her own.

IV. 4:40 P.M.

Alice is chopping vegetables for one of her Chinese specialties. "Who for?" Jackie demands on one of her frequent trips to the refrigerator (Delores has gone home; Jackie eats compulsively when bored). "Leah who?" she inquires pointedly when informed, though both of them know she knows only one Leah.

Probably you are supposed to chop the vegetables just before they go into the wok, but Alice wants to be able to relax with Leah, so she has decided to seal the pre-chopped vegetables into plastic baggies—much as she loathes the modern cook's wasteful dependence on plastic and aluminum foil and paper products, the heaps of garbage it creates—and store them in the refrigerator.

She is happy chopping vegetables and listening to a classical radio station. She certainly has no desire to see Theresa, who calls suddenly from West Fourth Street. Theresa with her opulent, tanned flesh, her shoulder-length black hair, who smokes and chews gum and talks fast all at the same time, who does her nails and wears a gold chain with her name in gold letters on it around her neck, who goes with disco music, not with Mozart.

"I just need to talk, and of course I thought of you. But tell me if it's a bad time." She sounds terrible; maybe she's even crying, though of course it's hard to tell with the pay phone crackling static and the A train thundering in on the upper level.

During Jackie's month at camp they had spent two nights together. On the first night Theresa was wildly responsive. *The young are so uninhibited these days,* thought Alice, who usually can't come with strangers.

"No, it's fine, come on over. I'm having company later, but right now I'm free." She hears herself hedging the bet, wonders why she's nervous. *You're perfectly safe after all; Leah's coming at 8:00, and you've got Jackie there in the other room.*

On their second night Theresa was again wildly responsive—until she started sobbing in Alice's arms. At first Alice, who had hoped to transcend her first-night inhibitions, was selfishly irritated. But she forgot such petty concerns in her panic when she heard Theresa say, "You're different from the others, I can tell. You actually care about me."

Ironic; in the bar, Theresa had been the one with the poise, the one who knew dance steps, how to handle a pool cue. Alice had thought she was getting away with something. Well, she learned. *See what you let yourself in for when you send your kid to camp for a few weeks. When you try to get something for nothing. Grow up, Alice.*

So here is Theresa at the door, wearing a tailored blouse and nice pants that make her look as though she might work in a bank. Jackie the ever-vigilant glares suspiciously; there is something wrong with the clothes, the hair. . . .

Theresa, for her part, hardly acknowledges Jackie. This seems odd; she had been so intrigued to learn Alice had a daughter. She'd pumped Alice for details: had she had natural childbirth, did it hurt a lot? Alice explained that natural childbirth had not been so popular in 1969; that even with anaesthetic it had hurt; but that nobody really remembers pain accurately after nine years, she'd had plenty of time to become a normal human being again. Looking back she sees she ought to have been on her guard right then. A lesbian mothers' C-R group she'd once belonged to had formulated a cardinal rule: beware of the prospective lover who's turned on by motherhood.

Heavy with misery, Theresa drops into a kitchen chair. Today she displays none of her previous social acumen. It is up to Alice to do everything: offer coffee, observe cheerfully, "You sounded so upset on the phone, I'm going to treat you to my best coffee beans," cover up the silence with the noise of the hand grinder. Finally it is even up to her to ask what's the matter.

"It's Mary. She's thrown me out." Theresa, who last month smoked Trues, dramatizes her predicament by taking a Camel nonfilter from her tooled leather cigarette case.

"But I thought you were planning on getting out anyway. I thought it was pretty much over between you two." On their second night Alice had learned plenty about Mary, older dyke, butch fatale, managerial woman. Her high-paid job in some branch of the money-manipulating industry, her Porsche, her vegetarianism, her goddess-worship, her villa in Puerto Rico, her apartment in Chelsea, her sudden interest in a nonmonogamous lifestyle.

"I didn't explain everything. What it is is, she's sort of been supporting me. Now she decides she wants to move that bitch in."

"Her other lover, the one you told me about?" The Camel smells wonderfully rich; Alice covets one.

"The designer."

"Theresa, I'm sorry."

"Oh god Alice, why can't I stop caring about her?" Theresa has an annoying way of flicking her cigarette lighter on and off as she talks. "I just can't understand how it could end like this."

"Didn't you see it coming?"

"And what was I supposed to do about it?" Injured, deprived of rightful sympathy, Theresa pouts, as Jackie does when she complains of a splinter and Alice advises her to wear shoes in the house.

"Have you been looking for work?"

"Oh, that." She dismisses crass materialism. "Sure, but doing what, waiting counter at Nedick's? Do you know I can't even type? I always thought if you're a girl and you learn how to type you'll never do anything else. I went to Brooklyn College for two years and I learned bullshit."

"Could you go back to school?" There's something wrong with her role here, Alice dimly senses. Shouldn't Theresa be able to think of all this?

"On what?"

"Wouldn't your parents help?"

"Maybe. Of course I'd have to move back to Brooklyn and go back in the closet totally. Do you know what my father would do if he ever suspected?" Theresa, despite the pout, is really quite attractive in this mood. Or perhaps it is the desperation of youth which, like the Camels, attracts Alice.

"Are you sure he doesn't?"

"Of course not. He'd beat the shit out of me."

"Theresa, he beats you?" Maybe it's serious then.

"He hasn't yet, but that doesn't mean anything. This is different. You don't know about Italian men, Alice. I had this friend, she got pregnant when she was only sixteen, her brother found out about it and he roughed her up so bad she lost the baby."

"Oh, I see." Attractive as youth may be, Alice is finding it difficult to sympathize with youth's problems, which are basically circumstantial. In five years they will have been worked through or outgrown. *And what about my problems?* By age thirty, one has excavated down to the hopeless bedrock of personality structure, has run smack into problems that will last the rest of one's life.

Besides, Theresa seems so eager to convince herself that her troubles are beyond solution.

"You're certainly in a tough spot," Alice agrees. "Don't you think, though, there must be some way out? Do you mind if I smoke one of your Camels?" *Take these delicious lethal cigarettes, she must smoke a pack a day, she doesn't even worry.*

"I don't know, sometimes I just want to get out of New York. Hitch to California, maybe, or even go to Alaska and learn to drive a truck or something. Just get out. This city is really shit, you know? And I keep thinking maybe someday something's really gonna happen, one of those natural gas tankers will explode or somebody'll bomb the—"

"Yes, I know it's for shit." Alice doesn't like this sort of talk, anymore than San Franciscans relish speculation about earthquakes. "But Alaska's pretty expensive and pretty homophobic. And L.A.'s a flat New York with a little more sunshine."

"At least I wouldn't have to worry about my family finding out. That's what bothers me the most. I can just see living there again, with them nagging me about when am I going to get a boyfriend and why don't I go to church."

"Is your family religious?" The Camel is making Alice dizzy, but she doesn't put it out. It tastes wonderful, tastes of the time when she was as young as Theresa (*but was I ever really quite so untogether?*) and had a nicotine stain on the index finger of her right hand.

"Well, they're Catholics, they go to church. I guess you could say my mother is religious."

"That must make it hard." Alice is working on a brilliant hunch: Theresa is hung up about being a lesbian. How quaint!

"Alice, would you mind telling me what *you* think I should do? And please don't tell me you're not me so you can't know what's right for me. That's what my therapist always says and it pisses the hell out of me."

"You're seeing a therapist?"

"Yes, but I may quit. I don't know where I'll get the money. Besides, she's seeing Mary."

Seeing Mary. Of course! Alice can place the whole scene: one of those incestuous circles, the therapist on a power trip, conflict of interest like crazy, no supervision. Theresa's in big trouble.

"Well, of course you'll have to make the ultimate decision about what's best for you. But first you have to get completely out of Mary's clutches. It sounds like she's done everything she can to make you totally dependent on her. You don't need that."

Theresa's face crumples. "She'd never do anything on purpose to hurt me. I know it."

"Maybe not, but you've still got to get away from her."

This obvious statement seems too much for Theresa. "Oh Alice," she wails, as though it explained everything, *"she brought me out."*

"You'll get over her." Despite Alice's intentions, it does not come out sounding kind.

"But you don't know." Theresa, sniffling, suddenly is unglamorous as hell. "She's the only one I've ever felt that way about. She's the only one I could ever come with, I mean I had to fake it with all the others, even you, I came closest with you, honest, but I just couldn't."

Alice is astounded, then indignant; men are to be treated this way, perhaps; women never. "Why in the world did you think you had to pretend?"

"Oh I'm sorry, I was afraid you'd be upset. It's just that people expect it, and I didn't want to have to explain. I guess I wanted to seem more sophisticated. It was completely different with Mary, I used to get so turned on."

"Yes. But this isn't the time to think about that." And Alice certainly doesn't want to hear the gory details.

"I guess it's silly, but I just can't imagine ever feeling like that about anybody else again."

"Of course, but you will. There's something I've been wanting to ask you, though. Do you suppose you feel guilty about being a lesbian?"

"What do you mean?"

"I mean that when you've got your whole family and the Catholic Church sitting in judgment, it must be a bit difficult to like yourself."

"I thought I told you." Theresa sounds annoyed. "I'm scared what my father would do if he found out. Also, I really don't want to hurt them. They *are* my parents, and they haven't had it easy. What does the Church have to do with it? I never really believed that crap, even when I was little it never made any sense. If God was good, what was hell for, anyway?"

"You're lucky, then." Alice, in her turn, is annoyed with Theresa. In fact she's beginning to wonder whether there's anything to be done for her. "I believed everything I was taught and then some. I used to lie awake worrying that maybe God wasn't really a Methodist like my parents. I thought for sure I'd burn for their mistakes."

Theresa gets out another cigarette; clearly she doesn't want to discuss religion. "Listen, I've been scared to ask you this. I hate to impose on people."

"Yes?" After this she must be gotten to leave somehow; it's late. *Your fifty minutes are up. Would you care to make another appointment?*

"Is there any chance I could maybe stay here for a little while? Just for a couple weeks till I get myself together."

Here it is: what you ought to have been afraid of. Think fast now. No. But why not? Because you would feel smoth-

ered. Because she would expect more, sex and money. Because you don't want to. But what to say to her? What Alice is seeing, formulating these reasonable objections, is Morgan's small, unkempt, roach-ridden apartment, perennial crash pad for everyone from neighborhood teenagers to underground fugitives.

"Look, Theresa, I'd have to think about it. Jackie just got back from camp, we've been having some trouble settling into our routine."

"I understand. The thing is, I have to get out by tonight, tomorrow morning at the latest. Mary's really been nasty these past couple days. I'm afraid she'll throw my stuff away or something."

"Do you have other possibilities? Couldn't you stay at your parents' for a week or two?"

"Not really, I can't keep moving in and out there. I do have a friend in the city but she's straight and she's got this guy living with her now."

"Theresa, I'm sorry, but I'm thinking it would be very difficult. Jackie doesn't adapt so well to third parties, and I'm a bit set in my ways myself." *I don't want to face your problems over breakfast.*

Theresa can't seem to take a hint. "I bet I'd get along fine with Jackie. I love kids; I could babysit when you go out."

"But there's still the problem of space. I've just gone on unemployment, and I'm around a lot."

"I know how to make myself scarce."

Not scarce enough. Alice is indignant; why should she be pushed? "Theresa, I'm sorry, I don't think it would work out."

Well, that is definite enough. "I suppose I'd better get going. I'm sorry I asked." Theresa's tone is a highly effective blend of hurt, disappointment and wounded pride.

"Not at all. You should always ask." *I will not be manipulated.*

"No, that's not what I meant. I mean I'm sorry I was wrong about you."

"Wrong in what way?"

"Like I told you, it's difficult for me to ask people for things. So I don't ask unless I think there's a good chance I won't be rejected."

"Now wait a minute." Alice knows defensiveness will be fatal, but she can't help herself. "I am really sorry to disappoint you, but I honestly didn't think it would work out. It's always better to be clear about these things from the start."

"Did you have to talk about *space*?"

"Space?" She's starting to feel crazy, unable quite to believe she's brought all this on herself in the privacy of her own home.

"You said the reason was space. Why couldn't you just say you didn't want me around? It's a drag, of course, especially when you're really depressed, to keep on finding out that people basically do not give a shit. But I'd rather not be lied to, all the same."

She gathers her things, resolute, *like a maid who's just been given notice,* Alice thinks. She's seeing herself the way she must look to Theresa: old and rich, powerful and together, in her clean sunny kitchen with the dried beans all lined up neatly in quart jars on the shelf, the politics forthrightly expressed in posters on the wall. A real hostess she is, able to offer fresh-ground coffee to a guest, able to offer advice. The kitchen is clean only because she just cleaned it, sunny only because the light is hitting just right, now, for an hour; but of course Theresa can't know that.

Alice thinks Theresa is going to go right out without saying anything, but she turns at the last minute, offers her hand. They shake, an odd gesture. Then Theresa says, "I'm sorry, Alice, I thought you were different."

Oh, it is a cheap shot, cheaper than Jackie's classic *you don't love me,* but effective. Alice, patsy, is left hollering down the stairwell, "Look, if you change your mind, if you want to talk, if I could help with anything. . . "

And here is Jackie, who can always spot Alice's lovers. "Mom, where did you know her from? How come you were having a fight?"

"We weren't having a fight," Alice lies. "Jackie, how many times do I have to tell you I can't stand it when you sneak around listening to my conversations?"

"I wasn't sneaking. I was just sitting."

"You were sneaking." Alice hates Jackie for making it so difficult for her to lead a normal adult life, but at the same time she understands. Jackie, being wholly at Alice's mercy, must needs look out for her own interests. *My god,* it suddenly registers, *how could I ever tell her I was pregnant?*

Going back to the kitchen, Alice notices with pleasure that Theresa has forgotten her Camels on the table.

V. 7:20 P.M.

If only Billie Holiday had been a dyke she'd have been really together. Alice can no longer remember which of her acquaintances once uttered this ridiculous statement, but neither can she play her Billie Holiday records without thinking of it. They are stacked on the machine now, along with her Bessie Smith records. *Bessie Smith, who was, sort of, and bled to death anyway, folks.*

Content, her house clean around her, Alice walks from room to room sipping wine. She is wearing a long cotton skirt which half-contradicts the statement made by her cropped hair. *Their pain on vinyl. Do I use their pain? Do I have the right?* But the doubt is only incidental; she can't help that she's happy, hearing their voices.

And how long since I've felt so relaxed before Leah? So I must be free now. Freer.

Reckless with wine, she decides to use the Tarot to confirm this. *If only Morgan the materialist could see me now.* The cards are in their traditional place in the drawer of the small night table by her bed. Seeing them smudged in places, some of the corners bent back, she wonders whether she ought to treat them more carefully, keep them wrapped in velvet as the books advise. But she is a busy woman, can't really afford the luxury of the occult; the powers that be, it seems to her, will just have to accept that fact.

At one time Alice believed she had a good intuitive grasp of the cards but, dilettante, she never studied them properly. Now she uses them so seldom that even her intuitions are blunted, rusty. Like a child who can't yet read the text, she's free to place her own interpretations on the pictures. And they do please her, the images of beautiful women she turns up, Strength, the Queen of Swords, the Nine of Pentacles. Picking the significator, she feels no suspense; it is almost an afterthought. Except that the card she turns over is the Devil, that hideous, mocking image, the hateful, naked little heterosexual pair chained at the foot of the throne. Bondage. Bondage to false ideas. *Well, you were fishing for compliments. See what you get?*

"What's that, Mom?"

Alice jumps. "For Christ's sake, Jackie, knock." One of the drawbacks of living in a railroad apartment is that there is always an excuse for a child to come barging through one's bedroom on the way to the front of the house.

"Sorry. What're you doing?"

"Haven't you ever seen my Tarot cards before?" Better for Jackie to have caught her smoking. "They're fortune-telling cards. I use them for fun sometimes."

"Oh, we studied that in school. It's a superstition."

The Tarot? Alice is offended. "Well, not quite. A superstition is like when you think it's bad luck if a black cat crosses your path, or Friday the 13th. . . . "

"It is so. Miss Gordon said fortune telling's a superstition."

"All right then, it's a superstition." *You're lucky I don't trundle you off to L.A. and sign us up for some wigged-out wicca cult.*

"Ooh, gross, that man and lady are naked." And Jackie skips off to her own room, whence the TV blasting at unacceptable levels announces she's trying to tune out Leah's arrival. Yet she dashes for the door the minute the buzzer rings.

"Did you know my Mom is superstitious? She does fortune telling."

"Why hello, Jackie. Is your Mommy at it again?" Leah stands there panting from the climb, half a pound of camembert in hand. Her exaggeratedly playful tone would perhaps have been suitable for a seven-year-old. Why can't she see it's an insult to the contemporary Jackie, with her tight jeans, her hands-on-hips stance, her studied adolescent flippancy? Alice, watching, is irritated, so she goes right back to the kitchen. But Leah follows almost immediately.

"Are you two speaking?"

Leah doesn't answer. She's looking good in jeans, a dark green corduroy jacket, a bright scarf knotted at her throat. *She is about to be a success* Alice thinks half-contemptuously, and not for the first time. *Five years at the outside.* She can already see the articles, the photographs of paintings: first *Ms.* and then the *Village Voice,* or maybe the other way around. Then a small piece in the *Times'* "Arts and Leisure" section.

"Would you like some cheap white wine? I'm afraid that's all I have." Despite chronic cash-flow problems, Leah usually manages to keep on hand a decent brand of whiskey. Style: that is the quality which, in Leah, covers a multitude of failings. *Whereas all I have is a certain tenacity.*

For example, Leah never cleans. When she and Alice lived together this was a disaster, the apartment a shambles, Alice critical, nagging. But now in Leah's cavernous loft the mess somehow disappears, everything seems as it should be, jungle of plants, odd sticks of furniture retrieved from other people's garbage, dust, clutter, paintings.

"I'd love a glass of wine. I've gone off the hard stuff for a while."

"Don't tell me you've reformed."

"Not voluntarily. Doctor's orders."

"Leah, why?"

"My stomach." She shrugs, embarrassed, half-pleased, maybe. "Nothing too significant, really. A precaution."

"Is success getting to you?"

"Alice, one lousy grant. It would keep a successful painter in the Hamptons for two months."

"All the same, I was jealous when I heard. In addition to being pleased for you, of course." Jealous, yes, as one might be to hear that one's ex-lover had finally moved in with someone. For all the time they had lived together Leah's painting had been at the bitter heart of their quarrels. *I am an artist. I belong tragically alone, making my art. Free of you and your snivelling brat I'd show what I could do* was not quite what Leah had ever said, but it was what she had felt, had ultimately acted on.

"Don't forget, I'm going to be forty in the spring. A grant, a show—it's not a hell of a lot, not at my age."

"Never mind that, how is your work going?" Alice the purist, the non-artist, means that this is what counts; money and fame shouldn't matter.

"Oddly enough, quite well."

"Fantastic."

"I'm actually a little afraid to talk about it, for fear of something going wrong. But it's as if I finally had the courage for all these things I've only imagined before."

"I'm glad." But really Alice is, for the moment, aghast at the stupidity, the sheer waste of their breakup. Of course Leah had needed a loft, but that was a technicality. She could have had everything she has now; they could still be together.

Naturally they'd had a few other problems; what they jokingly called their "interfaith relationship," for example. They made light of it ("my goyishe girlfriend," said Leah) and held feminist seders for which Alice, the better cook, made matzoh ball soup; but then they would get into terrible fights because Alice happened to make the wrong remark about Israeli foreign policy. It was not that Leah approved of Israeli foreign policy, either, but that Alice was somehow not authorized to express an opinion upon it.

There was also Jackie.

"And you, how do you like being on the dole? Better than working at that gruesome place, I'll bet."

"I don't know yet. I'm still too worn out to tell."

"Poor Alice. But I'm sure you'll bounce back within a couple of weeks; you have so much energy." Yes, Alice, the workhorse, the one with all the energy, the one who can stand shit jobs and motherhood. "Which reminds me, I was going to ask you whether you'd like to meet me in town tomorrow. I was planning on going to the Nevelson exhibit at the Modern."

"I wish I could. I've already promised Morgan I'd go to a demo tomorrow in New Jersey," Alice answers pointedly. She is tired of hearing about Art.

"Morgan the Commissar? You still see her?"

"Leah, please, spare me your animosities. Actually, I don't see much of her right now, but the demonstration is important and I'm going anyway. I'd like to go to a show with you sometime."

All of this, Alice notes with relief, is just comfortable sparring, nothing like the confrontations and acute pain of even six months ago. Stir-frying, she enjoys a vague anticipation of something pleasant. What is it, the wine, the prospect of a good dinner not eaten alone? The ritual examination of motives commences. *Am I safe, now, here, in this pocket of time? With food, with a friend I know well enough not to have to fear surprises? Is it true I don't have to worry right now, I'm okay, death doesn't matter even, or politics?* She doesn't know. She is just drunk enough to want to stand there forever over the wok, stirring, so that she makes the mistake of asking Leah to go tell Jackie it's time to say goodnight.

Leah reports back cold-eyed, furious.

"Her Highness desires me to inform you that she's planning to stay up and watch Starsky and Hutch."

Alice sees she has blown it with both of them. Her first impulse is to go and slug it out with Jackie, who knows she is not allowed to stay up and watch Starsky and Hutch, not even on a non-school night, not in this house. But then the food will get cold and there will be a knot in her stomach so she can't enjoy it, and Leah will only frown harder, withdraw further.

"I'm sorry, it was my mistake. I shouldn't have sent you in there."

"No, you shouldn't." Leah and Jackie always had such a strange involvement—an intricate dance of avoidance it was, really. Leah thought she had the worst of it. *Always being the one left over, not the real mother,* she said. Not seeing how torn Alice felt, how in the middle. *But do you really want a child?* Alice said. Of course it was the wrong question.

"Jackie still thinks about you a lot, you know. Every so often she'll mention you out of a clear blue sky, like the other day she said, 'Leah likes moussaka, doesn't she?' Then when I try to talk about you she changes the subject."

"I can understand that."

"I'm sorry, let's forget it, let's eat." Time enough to have it out with Jackie tomorrow.

Candles, a real tablecloth, the rice done just right. How pleasant to cook for someone, to eat with someone, to use chopsticks. *And perhaps I really will change, have the baby, learn all about protein complementarity and cook for my friends on food stamps. Rice, beans, whole wheat bread.* She imagines the apartment filled with light, with lives in motion, she the facilitator.

"Leah, do you ever feel you'd like to change your life?"

"In what way?"

"In any way. Don't you ever think about going someplace else and starting over?"

Leah considers, chopsticks poised in her slim fingers. Leah always eats slowly, delicately, as though thoroughly considering each bite. Alice gobbles.

"Sometimes I get sick of New York, like everybody else. But since I need to be here for my work I don't think about it that much. I just steer around the garbage cans, look the other way when I come down in the morning and find some old guy crashed out on my doorstep."

The wine is getting to Alice. "Sometimes, on a bus or something, I amuse myself making lists of all the things I still have time to do. *You still have time to become an ultra-left adventurist, rob banks, kill politicians, get life plus thirty. You still have time to learn to speak fluent Russian, Chinese, Swahili. You still have time to get a job in some godforsaken Midwest-*

ern town, wait tables, marry a truck driver, bear his children. Why is the idea that I *could* do those things important to me? I couldn't, really. They're not in character."

"Still, if you did, they'd be in character because you did them. Feminist art is art done by a feminist; what is in character for Alice is whatever Alice does."

"Really? I'm not sure. Remember how you used to talk about not having a child? You gave that reason: that having a child wasn't the sort of thing you would do."

"But of course I said that to make it easier on myself." Leah's matter-of-factness about this surprises Alice. "It was a choice, but at the time it was too painful for me to see it that way."

"Really? So you're past it. Good for you." Alice hesitates, then plunges. "To tell the truth, I've been thinking a lot lately about having another kid."

"Seriously?"

"Semi."

"Have you thought about how you'd handle it with Jackie?"

"Christ, Leah, how should I know?" But it is, of course, precisely the proper question. "Jackie's hardly a kid anymore, we seem more like a pair of roommates every day. How long am I supposed to keep making major life decisions on the basis of Jackie's needs?" This is an exaggeration; Alice has made few major decisions on the basis of Jackie's needs. It's all the minor ones made daily over the years that have worn her out, that constitute the real sacrifice. "The only thing you pledge yourself to when you have children is that you won't abandon them. It's not a monogamous relationship; you don't promise never to do it with anyone else."

"But Alice, why? I'm not saying you shouldn't; I just don't understand." Leah seems to be speaking out of simple friendly concern, and Alice is touched. Two years ago she'd have been too absorbed in her own ambivalences to respond this way.

"I've thought about it a lot, and I just don't know why. I've tried to forget about it, too, because it certainly would be a hell of a lot simpler. Jesus, I'd be fifty-five before I was through."

"Indeed. I think about that every time I go someplace and see all these grey-haired feminists with their last-chance babies. Why anyone would want to spend their late thirties changing diapers, their forties helping with homework. . . . "

"But all the same, I can't quite talk myself out of it. There's this image of me with the baby that keeps coming back. Thinking about it makes me feel free. Then I think maybe it's just a power trip, the idea of willing a life. Is that legitimate? I don't know, and I don't know how to find out, short of actually doing it."

"How would you do it, by the way?"

"You mean financially? Welfare, probably. I could always work off the books."

"No, I mean how would you get pregnant?"

"I have no idea. I mean, I have lots of ideas, ranging from medically-supervised artificial insemination to sleazy one-night stands. I'm sure if I want a baby I can manage it."

"What if it's a boy?"

Alice grimaces. "What a wet blanket you are. What if it has Down's syndrome, what if it has flippers instead of feet?"

"Oh Alice, I'm sorry. I don't mean to be obnoxious. I just want to say be careful. Funny things can happen with these decisions. At our age–"

"At our age what?" At thirty-three, Alice has never considered herself to be of an age with Leah.

"It's hard to get older and not have what you want. It's too easy to settle for the wrong thing. That's all I meant. I wish you the best, you know that."

"Leah, you understand I'm just telling you about this fantasy I have. I mean I haven't decided." Alice is frightened, like five-year-old Jackie, willful on a street corner, terrified suddenly when her mother would walk away.

"I understand."

"You're lucky, you know. You make something permanent. You can look at a roomfull of paintings and say:

there's my life. That is what I did. You get twice as much that way, your life doubled."

"Do I? I'm never quite clear about that."

"Don't you?"

"I think not. I always want it to be that way, but then there's the old anxiety. It doesn't matter what I painted yesterday. Am I still alive? Can I still paint? I never shake it. Do you know, it's given me this fucking ulcer, I'm sure it's not anything about 'success', it's just that. Can I still see? Can I still paint?"

"Well, I'm getting an ulcer too, Leah, and I don't paint." Alice is sorry now she mentioned the baby; she feels let-down, depressed.

"That's just my point. Maybe the same thing that's giving you your ulcer is giving me mine. Painting is a way of being alive, it involves all the same problems. You don't just do it once and for all. In fact I think the idea of the artist producing these great final objects is a very male thing."

"Leah, you know how skeptical I am about certain ideas being male and others female."

"Well, it makes sense. The first art was probably made by women, and it was made to be used. Can you imagine someone saying, 'Look, I made this piece of pottery, now I'll retire, I can live forever'? Of course not. It's men who spend their lives building pyramids, tombstones, monuments. In the end, of course, it's pure chance that anything survives. Some pots do, some cave-paintings, some pyramids. *We* certainly don't."

Alice, socialist-feminist, doesn't like to admit she's a bit intrigued by a theory which smacks of matriarchist tendencies. "And where does worldly recognition fit in? Doesn't getting a grant help you feel you've done something worthwhile?"

"Of course it helps. A necessary illusion, a curtain against the outer darkness. It's pleasant to be told you've done well, but it doesn't really change anything."

"Are you saying there's no hope then?" Alice smiles.

"Maybe. This will probably seem pretty silly in the morning."

"Yes. Let's finish the wine."

Late, Alice embraces Leah at the door, then stands behind it listening to her descending footsteps. *How odd there's nothing in the least sexual left.* For if there were, surely it would have surfaced this evening, with all the wine and speculative talk. No, that thinness, those elegant bones, are good for nothing now except to look at. What Alice wants is superabundance of flesh. Even Theresa was a step in the right direction.

What were we doing together at all, for that matter? Such an unlikely pair. The realization that she really can't remember just brings back all the old pain of loss, the ache in the vanished limb. *Leah, Morgan. Do we become purer, harder as we grow older, more different from each other, more fixed in our separate personalities?* It is a grand idea, but it chills her. *I'll call Leah soon,* she promises herself, *maybe there's something coming up next month at the Whitney.*

Turning, her eye is arrested by the absence of a familiar irritation; "Today Is The First Day Of The Rest Of Your Life" is missing from Jackie's door. It takes her a minute to notice the small square of paper, folded many times, taped in its place. On the face of this is printed, in letters so tiny they seem to challenge her to locate the message, not "Mom," but her name.

The text is in Jackie's new, laborious script. "I'm sorry I said I was going to stay up and watch Starsky and Huch and I didnt. I cleaned my room too. Will you give me a kiss. I hope you had a plesent evening with Leah." The room Alice tiptoes into is rather unnaturally neat.

At first inclined to smile at the psychology of children, Alice remembers the poster. She hunts for it with mounting urgency, as though it were important, finally locates it in the obvious place, the wastebasket, crumpled though not torn. But much too wrinkled to be resurrected.

She did this for me. I'll talk to her tomorrow. I'll get her another, she can put it up anywhere, on the refrigerator if she wants to. Alice, frightened, is very nearly angry, as mothers are when children dart out into the street in the path of cars, put themselves in any danger. Then, seeing how Jackie lies drawn up on the bed in the defensive posture of fetuses and nursing home patients, pity and terror claim her. *I made her. I made her. How can I betray her?*

Alice drinks a glass of water, takes a vitamin pill, flosses her teeth to forestall gum disease, lies in bed alone. Hard to sleep, but she'd better. She'll be hungover; Jackie will wake her early.

So then there is this person in bed with her. She cannot see the face but hears what the voice says. Obeys directions. And her hand moves down.

Rockabye and good night go to sleepy little baby.

Alice sleeps, enters the first circle of dreams.

Yellow Jackets

for Phyllis Shannon Clausen, who told me stories

Month: July. Time: evening. Place: the outskirts of a small midwestern town. Picture a squat, square, ugly red brick house. On its screened-in porch two old women, neighbors, sit: the guest, Mrs. Frederick Baxter (Gertrude), heavily rocking; her hostess, Mrs. Joseph Biehler (Laura), by her own fault suffering in the straight-backed chair. *I've sworn for twenty years I'd buy another; will I die without seeing two comfortable chairs on my porch?*

From a curtained window weak light leaks over the yard; there is a ragged heave of lawn toward the unsidewalked street. Fill in a background of insect noise; low, furtive-seeming murmurs of passersby; infrequent flash of headlights. Remember the heat, always the heat, so basic that it almost goes unnoticed: a fact, dimension, condition of this existence, indelible as depression or dangerous fever.

The morning all undone, over and over, every day I woke, the neat package of evening all untied that gave me such satisfaction when I'd washed up from supper and the children were in bed. Oh, morning is a terrible time, the time of unmaking, and yet I believe I still loved morning best, icehats on the milk bottles, the cold cold clink of them; coffee, and Joe just getting started in his truck. I who am finished, undone; I who ought to be ready.

Like flies around a pot of strawberry jam, she is saying. Or yellow jackets, more like yellow jackets. A bunch of yellow jackets round the table at those family picnics in the county park. Such pesky creatures, moving off a little when you'd shoo them, then coming right back. And all that food, you know how it is with the Germans.

I know just what you mean, Mrs. Baxter sympathizes, about yellow jackets. We had them something awful on the Fourth this year.

Once, Mrs. Biehler continues, when Mavis was three, she tried to catch a yellow jacket and it bit her. I'll never forget her screaming, and the heat, and Joe's mother scowling at me. I must have been expecting Joey, too, at the time; I recall feeling quite nauseous. This was unusual for Mavis, she was generally so quiet, much more so than Joey of course (*poor little Joey*), or even Lucille (*marrying as she did*). Till finally I lost my temper and slapped her good.

Mrs. Baxter allows she's glad the Fourth's over with. She is always happy, of course, to see the children; but she gets so tired.

The children, snorts Mrs. Biehler, the children indeed. *A string of female names: Mavis and Lucille; Jo Ellen, Maxine, Rosemary, Mona.* At first I thought it was just coincidence, them all of a sudden buzzing and swarming and pestering me to death. *Mavis in Minneapolis, Lucille in Los Angeles, Jo Ellen in Madison, Rosemary in Des Moines, Maxine you never know from week to week, Mona in my spare bedroom, not moaning yet.* Just another stage, as Mavis always claimed when hers were little.

Well, this is what we have to expect at our age, Laura, Mrs. Baxter mentions. This is what we have to look forward to. From here on I suppose even third and fourth cousins will be showing an interest. At least I can be grateful for my Charlotte.

But that's not it with me, Gert, Mrs. Biehler points out, trying hard to be tactful. Lucille, of course, is quite nicely fixed up. And even Mavis does well with her settlement. No, it isn't money, it's how they look at me, all these expensive long distance phone calls and sudden visits. It's Maxine coming down for the weekend, it's Jo Ellen driving all the way from Madison to play that tape for me when I'd told her plain enough I didn't want to hear it. It's Rosemary going through my cupboards.

Did she do that? Mrs. Baxter eagerly cries. My Charlotte would never.

She certainly did, confirms Mrs. Biehler, grim. And no permission asked. Granny, she says to me, like a little girl all excited, this is Depression Glass! It ought to be, I says, I got it in the Depression.

See what I mean, that stuff is worth money now, Mrs. Baxter nods.

You know how I feel, her friend continues, I feel just like some beat-up old dress that they fish out of the fifty cents bin at the Goodwill and hang up on the antiques rack for fifty dollars. Just because I have lasted. *And I won't even speak of Maxine, with her hair chopped off like you'd cut it with a lawn mower, and calling herself Mavisdaughter when her name is Larson, never mind what unpleasantness her father has caused.*

Can't they see, Mrs. Baxter laments, that a person's got little enough to keep them while they're alive and bury them decently, after? Don't they have eyes? But no. They figure better safe than sorry, I suppose. Calling up to ask would I like to be read to! Oh, I am grateful for Charlotte.

Even Lucille has started in, admits Mrs. Biehler, Lucille, who never was a whiner. Writing me letters on her artistic note paper: Wouldn't you like to come out for a little vacation, maybe spend the winter? Arthur and I will be happy to send the tickets. Though perhaps she feels guilty, dumping Mona on me. *A funny, sullen little thing, Mona.*

Well, why not go, says pragmatic Mrs. Baxter. After all, Los Angeles.

I've been already, Mrs. Biehler reminds her. Oh, it is true I haven't seen my grandson in seven years. *In his pictures he slightly appears to resemble my Joey.*

David? Mrs. Baxter's interest quickens. What's David doing these days?

I cannot say I am fond of California, Mrs. Biehler firmly continues, preferring to disregard the question. *You wouldn't want to know, Gran, was what Mona answered me when I asked her how he is filling up this year he took off from college. Joey dead already, at his age.* Besides, Gert, don't you see what I'm getting at?

No, Laura, what? begs plodding Mrs. Baxter.

That it is only another form of pestering on the part of Lucille and them, her friend concludes, triumphant. Would you care for some cake? I'm afraid it's only Sara Lee from the supermarket.

In this heat, Laura? I've lost my appetite. But I'll have a spot of iced tea, if you can spare it.

Of course, says Mrs. Biehler, reach me your glass.

Oh don't get up, she cries reflexively; but her comparatively spry hostess is already well on her way to the kitchen.

I take Sweet 'n Low, she therefore hollers out.

Goodness, Gert, after all these years don't you think I'd remember? Mrs. Biehler's voice continues through the open window, over a clink of glasses.

And even Mavis she says (*good little Mavis*), who's supposed to be taking courses to keep her busy, comes around here all at loose ends asking is there anything she can do. Reminds me of rainy days when the children were little. How I dreaded rain! You ought to be growing up on the farm like me, I'd tell them, you'd never ask what to do. Then I'd make Mavis dust, or iron handkerchiefs. *Moving through those high, light rooms on Chestnut Street. How I loved those rooms.* Lucille, most often, could think up some game to play, and of course there wasn't much work for a boy around the house, so Joey got off easy. Here's your iced tea, Gert. Have you been following this in the papers about how Sweet 'n Low is supposed to cause cancer?

At our age, Laura, what difference can it make? Mrs. Baxter calmly reasons, getting a firm grip on the sweating glass. Besides, I tend towards diabetes. Perhaps you're right; it's something other than money yours are after.

No, it's not money they're after, with all their pestering. *Oh, she has a poor opinion of my daughters, Lucille marrying a Jew, and Mavis, of course, being divorced now.* Do you find you feel the heat worse as you get older? I believe I do. *And of all five grandchildren, not a one like her Charlotte, married to an electrician, maybe, but so helpful, so sweet.*

I'm sure I do, affirms Mrs. Baxter. And don't it look like this spell would last forever? Maybe we'll get some rain tonight, though. So Mona is staying the summer, is she now?

Yes, her friend replies, concealing considerable uneasiness. *Mona is going through a difficult time, Lucille wrote.* Yes, she has decided.

Mrs. Baxter observes that it must be a trial, having someone always under foot like that.

Well, I can't say she's any help to me, but she keeps herself to herself. She's no hindrance, either, like some people I could mention. *She is extremely secretive and does not want to discuss her problems with me, Lucille went on. Of course the end of high school is often a difficult time for today's youngsters, so I don't worry.* Although she smokes, such a terrible filthy habit. *Perhaps spending a few weeks with you will give her the opportunity she needs to get herself on a better footing.* But it's good to know there's someone in the house, if anything should happen.

I know what you mean, Mrs. Baxter agrees quickly. Why, ever since poor Winifred's accident seems like I've been afraid to so much as go down cellar for a jar of jam. Is it because of Arthur that you prefer not to go to Los Angeles?

Mrs. Biehler assures her that's water under the bridge. *Though I will admit neither Joe nor I were happy when Lucille came home one day and announced she would be marrying this Arthur Moskowitz, a would-be college professor from Chicago.* Arthur is a good man, she emphasizes. The Jews are fine people. *And how we argued, Lucille reminding me that Father tried to stop me marrying Joe. But this is different, I tried to make her see.*

You may be right, I'm sure, concedes Mrs. Baxter, but something like this you never really quite get over, all the same. Take when my Eula married that twice-divorced fellow, and her not out of high school.

Yet look what came of it, Mrs. Biehler cries. *With us, I told her, it was following the War, and of course there was still considerable feeling against the Germans. But at least Joe was a Christian, and not a Roman Catholic either. I would not have married a Catholic.* Didn't Eula have Charlotte by that man? Could you ask for better than Charlotte? *Though I can never rightfully blame Lucille, after what I almost did. It was just she came so close on Joey, and I was tired.*

Of course Charlotte is a comfort, assents Mrs. Baxter. Still—poor Eula. How hard it is to watch your children suffer.

Oh isn't it, isn't it, Mrs. Biehler mourns. *I went so far as to get the name of a St. Paul doctor that did such things. Worried half to death thinking how I could keep it from Joe. In the end, of course, I couldn't get the money.* To think of my mother, who buried three of us, not counting the one or two that was born dead. *Where Lucille is concerned, I feel I have only myself to blame.* I don't suppose I'll ever get over Joey. I know Joe never did. *Though our church no longer holds that it is a sin.*

You never really do, Mrs. Baxter agrees.

When Joe passed away, last thing he called for Joey. *There are times now I feel I should have had more than the three.* And he looked up, and there was Lucille standing. You know how tall she is. And confused, like he was, he decided she was Joey. So he was satisfied, anyway.

I am glad to know Joe went easy, Mrs. Baxter says. I surely wish the same for my poor Fred.

Have you been to see him? her friend makes ritual inquiry. *But who could have guessed there'd be another War? So young Joey looks in his uniform in that picture.*

Yes, sighs Mrs. Baxter, yesterday. He was asleep, though; they tell me he sleeps the better part of the time. Even when he's awake he don't know me, of course. Poor Fred.

At least he is not in pain, observes Mrs. Biehler, rather troubled. *I so much did not want to be like Mother.*

Mrs. Baxter agrees that this is a blessing; ventures, after a moment, that it seems to be cooling off a little and perhaps she would have a piece of the cake that was mentioned.

By all means, says Mrs. Biehler; I'm happy to get it out of the house. I tend to nibble, and I shouldn't have it, not with my weight. I keep telling Mona not to buy it. Of course she's thin as a rail.

Your weight, scoffs Mrs. Baxter. Laura, look at me!

Oh, go on, Gertrude! (but Mrs. Biehler is pleased). I'm fatter than I look, it's just I know how to dress. And how is your blood pressure these days? What does the doctor say?

About the same, Mrs. Baxter admits, taking a forkful of cake. Of course I'm on the medication still. This cake really is not bad at all for store bought. But maybe you should get Mona to make you a nice coffee cake from scratch. Charlotte does that for me sometimes, it's not so much trouble.

I'm afraid Mona is perfectly useless in a kitchen. *You'll see soon enough, it's different, I said to her. It's different with a little one, there's no getting around it.* To tell you the truth, I'd rather not turn her loose in there. Who knows what sort of mess she'd make?

At least, Mrs. Baxter hints broadly, she might learn a thing or two she will need to know one day.

Perhaps; but I'm not running a cooking school. Let Lucille teach her, with her Chinese cooking lessons, since pot roasts and simple baking like I showed my girls seems to be insufficient, Mrs. Biehler replies rather bitterly.

Chinese? Mrs. Baxter raises heavy eyebrows.

Chinese, repeats Mrs. Biehler. Fifteen dollars a lesson, I think she wrote it cost her.

Well, says Mrs. Baxter, shaking her head in sympathetic sorrow, she's got that kind of money, I suppose.

Mrs. Biehler is reminded somehow of her other problems. Did I tell you Maxine showed up over the weekend, not bothering to telephone? she inquires. And Jo Ellen was here with her tape machine, after I made it clear I wasn't interested? Maxine did not look at all pleased when she saw Jo Ellen.

What's this, cries Mrs. Baxter, they don't get along?

Apparently not, admits Mrs. Biehler. I asked Mavis about it; I'll explain later. Anyway, they have this thing called the Women's Something-or-Other Project, something to do with history, over there at the University where Jo Ellen is trying to get tenure.

Trying to get *what?*

That's all right, Gertrude, Mrs. Biehler reassures her, I wouldn't know of it myself if Arthur hadn't been through it. *Two professors in the family now.* It means the teacher has a permanent job, can't be fired.

Why, what an outlandish idea! marvels Mrs. Baxter. What if they stopped showing up to work?

Mrs. Biehler allows she never thought of that. It does sound kind of funny, she concedes, but Jo Ellen explained it to me, how it's important for freedom of speech and such. Anyway, she wants it awful bad. And she says it's harder for a woman to get it.

Like everything else, Mrs. Baxter generalizes. But then, of course the men would need the jobs most. Do you suppose Jo Ellen will ever get married?

Who knows? Here I will be seventy-eight in October. *And Mona's condition I cannot even mention.* Mrs. Biehler looks so upset that Mrs. Baxter, alarmed, tactfully returns the conversation to the subject of Jo Ellen's tape recorder.

Well, she explains, apparently this project involves Jo Ellen going around tape recording women our age talking over their memories. From what she told me, it isn't helping her get that tenure she wants, since the higher-ups say she should be writing articles about books by men.

Some people don't know which side their bread's buttered on, Mrs. Baxter observes pointedly.

My thought exactly, her friend agrees. Jo Ellen, I told her, I think you are being foolish. I think you had better make up your mind, do you want this tenure, or not? But she didn't answer me; she just laughed and turned on that machine, though I had informed her several times I wasn't interested.

And what was on it? Mrs. Baxter is perhaps too eager.

A woman talking, replies Mrs. Biehler with distaste. Though she had such a thick accent (Polish, I would judge) that it was hard to understand her. First she told about places she had worked in, filthy sweat shops and such. Then she got real personal, and went on about having relations with her husband and all, and the times her babies were born. *It made me nearly sick to hear it, thinking of Mother.* Perhaps the Poles don't mind discussing such things, but I could never. *I promised myself I'd never be like her, with a belly like an old sack of potatoes, and always so tired.*

You mean you want me to say a bunch of stuff like that, and then you are going to play it for total strangers? I asked Jo Ellen. *One time I remember watching for the Doctor, I couldn't have been more than six or seven, hearing her, praying so hard for him to hurry. Praying to see him riding up that road.* But she claims many women are glad to talk to her. They start remembering things they'd all but forgotten, she tells me. *Hearing her moan and scream in that back room; too many of us, by then, to be sent to the neighbors.* They're so glad to have somebody to talk with, according to Jo Ellen.

Well, I says, I'm not so hard up, thank goodness. Even if I did have such frightful things to tell. And as for what people have forgotten, sometimes they have their reasons. But we need your stories, Granny, Jo Ellen starts in, like a youngster begging for candy.

If that ain't the limit! Mrs. Baxter exclaims.

I could have slapped her, Mrs. Biehler agrees. I could see she was getting impatient with me, too, though she was trying not to show it. Do you keep a diary, Granny? she says to me. Of course not, I says, what earthly good would that be? *Not mentioning my flower garden journal, which I've never showed anyone.* Your life isn't just your private property, you know, she says. *Looking at me with that same covetous look Rosemary had when she spied the set of Bauer dishes I have in the cupboard, the ones I use for everyday, and she said to me, Granny, do you know, they sell a plate like this for ten dollars in the shops in Des Moines?*

Whose property is it, then, I'd like to know? I inquired of Jo Ellen. And what would you young women want with it anyway? You're liberated, you don't need my stories. Don't you have jobs and TV dinners and frozen waffles and Pampers and ways to get out of having babies, for that matter? Don't you have tenure? I said to her.

Not yet I don't, she answered me back. And then Maxine had to get into it. It's Granny's story, she informs Jo Ellen. She shouldn't have to talk if she doesn't want to.

Of course not, Jo Ellen says, with that phony smile. Well, Granny, I think I will take my tape machine and go. I have quite a drive back to Madison, after all.

Maxine was prepared to stay the night. But I was so worn out with their bickering, I wanted to be quiet. So I reminded her Mona was using the spare room. *I will write them a letter, Gran, she said to me, but I would like to remain here till the end of August.* I had a headache from listening to all that, and my arthritis was bothering me something dreadful. *Mona, I said, you've got to listen to reason.* Mona, of course, is so quiet it's almost like being alone. *Are you telling me I should get rid of it, Gran, because I'm not going to, Mona said. Not this time. Don't worry, I'll go home before I start to show, your neighbors won't know a thing.* But later, when Mavis called, I asked her about the girls.

And what is the problem between them? Mrs. Baxter interjects, feeling rather out of her league but desirous of conveying sympathy.

According to Mavis, Mrs. Biehler explains, Jo Ellen calls herself a radical feminist, whatever that may be. *They are used to little bastards in L.A., said Mona.* But she is still willing to associate with men under some circumstances. *Young lady, I mentioned, kindly watch your language.*

I should hope so, Mrs. Baxter observes, or how can she expect to meet a future husband? What about Maxine?

Well, elaborates Mrs. Biehler, Maxine, according to Mavis, is more radical even than that. *In '34 when they had that terrible strike, Joe was all set to go up to Minneapolis.* Though it was plain enough to me she didn't much care to discuss it. *Full of swagger, and talk about the Working Man.* While Rosemary, Mavis claims, is not the least bit radical. *Oh, how I had to beg him not to go, as later I begged Joey.*

In my day, I hinted, a radical meant a Red. *Joe, please Joe, we have a chance, I said, we have a chance.* I hope, I said to Mavis, that neither Jo Ellen nor Maxine are doing anything foolish. *And I was right, in the long run, wasn't I?*

Oh goodness, no, Mother, don't worry about that, says Mavis. *We got this place all paid for, didn't we? And Doctors and Professors in the family, for what they're worth. Though Joe had to slave for others all his life.*

I let Mavis know I'm aware Rosemary has been living with her young man. I didn't know you knew, she says, embarrassed.

Of course I knew, I says. Just because I may wear bifocals doesn't mean I'm completely blind, not yet. I know how the young people tend to think these days, and I made a couple inquiries of Jo Ellen.

I hope they get married soon. I think it is likely, said Mavis (*always the good one*) in that little voice of hers, like I might hit her, though I never struck the children. *Not like Mother, making us cut the switches.*

I don't really see why she should, Mavis, I pointed out, considering the example she has to look to. *Who could have imagined, when Mavis married a Doctor, he'd end unzipping his pants in front of little girls in schoolyards?*

Mother, please, says Mavis, so sensitive. *And Joe so proud of her, on their wedding day.*

And where does Maxine come by her means of support? I took the opportunity to inquire, being that we were on the subject of the children. Mavis, I figured, was probably giving her money. *Mavis, good; but softer than biscuit dough.*

Oh, Mavis said, she is presently looking for work. She and her friend Cindy share their income.

That's odd, isn't it, I said. Two girls.

Here Mrs. Baxter, used to these harangues, ventures she wouldn't mind another smidgen of that cake. I can see what you're saying about that tape machine, she quickly adds. It would be an embarrassment.

Oh, indecent, indecent. I never could have done it, says Mrs. Biehler.

But then, she muses, you wouldn't be obliged to tell about anything you didn't want to.

Gertrude Baxter! Mrs. Biehler protests.

Well, she confesses, it would give a person someone to talk to. I'm not like you, Laura, I don't enjoy being alone.

But what about Charlotte? urges Mrs. Biehler.

Charlotte is sometimes busy with those two babies. Besides, there are a few things I'd like to preserve for future generations.

Such as, Gertrude? the other prompts, severely.

Recipes, Mrs. Baxter defensively murmurs, recipes and things.

Recipes! Recipes is hardly the kind of thing Jo Ellen would want to hear about, Mrs. Biehler is driven to explain. *I did not tell her I write about my flowers.* If you've got recipes, hand them down to Charlotte.

But these aren't ordinary recipes, they're fancy, things my mother taught me special, pleads Mrs. Baxter. She didn't teach none of my sisters, only me. And Charlotte, while being a good cook, is only a plain cook. Besides, I doubt that she would have the time. That husband of hers, you know, can be quite demanding.

But don't you see, Mrs. Biehler cries, thoroughly exasperated, that cooking is just the sort of thing young women like Jo Ellen have absolutely no time for or interest in? *You'll see soon enough, I told Mona, how things will change. Babies require a clean place to play, after all, and clean clothing, and food to eat, which can't come out of a jar forever.* Aren't you aware that this is what they think is wrong with us, that we spent too much time cooking and cleaning and having babies? *You shouldn't have them if you plan not to lift a finger, I said to her, after all you needn't, abortion is perfectly legal, I read the papers.* Of course they haven't the faintest notion what it was like for us, no washing machines or daycare. No mixes or Sara Lee packaged cake back then, for sure.

Calm down, Gran, it's bad for your heart, Mona said. And there's something in her voice that calms me, I don't know what.

But have you ever stopped to consider? I said. Do you find the answers in your Buddhist books?

Hey Gran, she said, with her funny little smile. And I do believe I prefer the way she calls me Gran to the others, with their Granny, Granny, Granny, like I was one of those silly dustmop dresses, or a pair of spectacles. She stubbed out her cigarette and she took my hand, all aching and twisted up with the arthritis, and laid it on her stomach, that's still as flat as flat, though not for long.

Never mind about the cooking and the cleaning, she said. Let's don't borrow trouble, okay, Gran?

What a funny, old-fashioned thing for her to say.

Well, of course I would have no way to know all this, being that there are no university professors in my family, replies Mrs. Baxter with considerable dignity. Since the young women of my acquaintanceship seem content to have babies like everybody else. But would you simply mention my name to Jo Ellen?

Mrs. Biehler regards her disapprovingly. *I'm seventy-seven and still not ready to die.*

You might tell her I will give her some additional information, if only she will record my recipes, Mrs. Baxter insists.

I will mention it, Mrs. Biehler concedes at last (*I have had it so much easier than my mother, how is it I am still not satisfied?*), helping herself to a generous slice of cake.

Three-Part Invention

La, tout n'est qu'ordre et beauté. . . *
—Charles Baudelaire, *L'Invitation au Voyage*

HEATHER,
her brown foot naked on the accelerator. Don't drive barefoot, Mother always said; but it feels good like this, all muscles connected. August, and the lust for summer on her; heat played off against the cool clean memory of river. Shift up, then up again, merging. Freeway nearly clear yet, no hint of rush-hour traffic. Cloudless, yes, but minus mountains today: only brown-grey sky above the vague mass of hillrim to her left. *Did we always have this, this haze?* Distressing question. She reaches, turns up the music. Top forty sounds fine on the freeway, and she loves freeways, being a good driver. Immortal, she feels, in moments, knowing her power. Gas shortage will come, strip her, they say, of this pleasure; but she's a good driver now.

Get down, get down, get down, pleads the radio.

PAM
Get down, Kyla.

She hears herself scream this over a burst of submachine fire. The guerrillas approach one kilometer nearer the outskirts.

JOYCE
covers machine, pokes card into metal slot. Click: 5:03. And life commences, simple. Or not so simple, given that she's

* There, there is nothing but order and beauty. . .

tired, given it's her night to cook. Not to mention imminent exile from the air conditioning.

Good night, good night, good night, say all the women.

HEATHER

Hearing an unfamiliar sputter rise to dominate the chorus of engine noise, she snaps off the radio to listen. Traffic has thickened, she notes. Tieup on bridge.

Damn the damn car, she curses, wondering will it make Seattle. *Damn the fucking car, and what they pay me at the lab.*

Though all such nuisances are now temporary, of course.

PAM

"Get down, Kyla."

Outside, brown boys vindictively heave firecrackers into the dry gutters beneath scraggy palm trees, dodge behind subtropical fringe. Kyla, small for seven, kneels facing backwards on the torn front seat.

"And while you're at it, roll up that window, please."

Kyla frowns, wrinkles her little freckled nose, pops gum. "What if I don't want to?"

JOYCE

stands sweating in the stopped train, bodies packed close around her. So close you might not fall if you passed out. Hardly the time to contemplate that, however, trapped here under the East River in the cattle cars. She wills herself to concentrate on newsprint. UNEMPLOYMENT UP, says the *Guardian.*

She hates this, yes. But others have to live it.

PAM

"Look, Kyla, just do it. Any minute one of those firecrackers'll come sailing through the window."

There was this Russian woman who said or wrote somewhere that the serious revolutionary must not have children.

Seven is an awfully young communist.

HEATHER
parks in the vast Fred Meyer lot. Slips into sandals; glides, weak with hunger, across burning blacktop, conscious of her body, her tanned smooth legs in cutoffs. Inside, the air is edged with an expensive chill, the Muzak soothing as Darvon; heaps of avocados, pyramids of brie in the cheese section herald plenty. Here's wealth untold, here's heavy opulence, here's all the grandeur of shopping in a football stadium. Heather, suburb born and bred (in one of her earliest memories she's three, screaming, trapped in a speeding grocery cart, reckless Pammy at the helm), of course thinks nothing of it. She wanders meditatively up this aisle and down that; settles, finally, on a Florida grapefruit, carton of cottage cheese, expensive pint of blueberries for dessert.

Here's famine amid plenty. She plans to lose five pounds before the wedding.

PAM
leaves the battered Dart parked at a reckless angle, trails Kyla up broken concrete steps to the fallingdown stucco apartments, two "mission-style" stories set around a dry, weedy courtyard. The stucco's that hideous shade which the Crayola people label "flesh," though Kyla wouldn't know it, Connie having removed this item from her crayon collection.

"Christ, Pammy, LA's ugly," Joyce had commented, in her unthinking critical fashion, like Mother's. "Didn't you and Connie like Oakland better?" She had to say this, yes, knowing their reasons.

Pam had said nothing, hadn't even protested that gratuitous "Pammy."

JOYCE
turns the key in the final lock, at last gets the fucking door open. Here's Alan, harassed as a housewife, with Leah on his arm.

"Sorry I'm late. The trains were all screwed up."

"That's okay." But she knows how he hates to rush. Now he will be late to study group.

"Check her pants," he cautions in parting. "I think she made. There's a letter for you in on the kitchen table."

HEATHER
eases into the wide, winding street that fronts the low apartment complex: duplexes, really, set back in folds of greenery that more or less obscure their cheap, discolored siding. She shares her unit with Candace, who is, thank god, out of town, and will shortly become irrelevant.

She pulls up alongside the row of silver mailboxes, slides over, rolls down the window. No check, but a letter from Brooklyn.

She sits in the driveway skimming it, biting her lip.

PAM,
somehow balancing the two sacks of groceries, checks the mailbox before going up. Surprise, surprise, there's actually a letter. *One the Feds didn't get,* she thinks wryly, automatically checking the closure for evidence of resealing.

JOYCE
"St. Pam in Los Angeles," Joyce is complaining to Jake, her cleaver busy with the Chinese cabbage.

Jake, housemate, anti-nuclear activist, laid-back beneficiary of unemployment, sits now at the kitchen table, Leah on his lap. Somehow he manages to ignore her ominous grumbling, the hostile gesture with which she hurls toy after toy away from her onto the grubby linoleum; but Joyce, prescient parent, braces herself for howls of rage.

"Well, you know ultraleftists," he remarks quite cheerfully.

"Jake, she's my sister," snaps Joyce. She, too, is in a bad mood tonight.

PAM
hoists catlitter, wheatflour, rice, beans, oranges, oil, canned tomatoes; begins the ascent, Kim hollering from above, "Hurry up, Pam, I gotta pee *real bad.*"

That letter, in the heavy, square, expensive envelope postmarked Portland, must somehow be from Heather.

JOYCE

"Ionizing radiation," Jake's explaining. "Half-life. . . millirems. . . radon daughters. . . " He appears almost to pronounce these terms with pleasure, delighted by the technical precision of which the language is capable.

Joyce cooks. Posted above the stove by way of benediction is, of course, no "Bless Our Happy Home," no little fake sampler of sentimental verse extolling the kitchen's charms, but the War Resisters League's "Nuclear America" map, pinpointing plants and targets.

"Radon daughters. Why radon *daughters*?" she quibbles. If you say the words, will the words help? There are two states of being, or so she's always seen it. What is called reality; then this terror.

HEATHER

rinses the river out of her new swimsuit, steps into the shower, soaps her hair. Should she shave her legs? She does see Gordon tonight. But he'll be tired, and she with her empty stomach. . . .

Emerging, she just makes out her flesh well-tanned, her breasts white circles in the steamy mirror. *I'll be exactly twenty-five years old.* It seems a likely age to take this step. Look: only a very few stretch marks on her thighs from when she was fat in college.

But goddamn Joyce, superior bitch of a sister. *"Of course you know my views on the institution of marriage."* Imagine making your child a bastard on purpose!

JOYCE

Leah squalls now in earnest; Joyce appeases. She does feel ghastly tonight. Premenstrual, she might think, if it weren't for. . . Right.

PAM
sits rolling a cigarette in the small livingroom of crooked venetian blinds, dust, broken chairs, ancient records in orange crates. The most functional-looking item is the mimeograph machine occupying an alcove, as though this were '68 or the days of the Tsars; on it the New Communist Party prints its internal memos and rush leaflets.

Third World faces surround her: Che, Malcolm X, Madame Binh. "Whattsa matter, don't your mama like white folks?" a sharp neighborhood child had asked Kyla one afternoon, looking around at the posters.

In fact, neither Pam nor Connie is Kyla's mother. Kyla's a gift, The Child Who Came to Dinner; Kyla's a survivor. Her mother, crazy, and crazier on acid, tried to drown her in the bathtub at eighteen months.

Pam, cigarette-fortified, approaches Heather's letter.

JOYCE
sets out the wok, places the bowl piled high with chopped vegetables beside it. Thinking she'll just sit down for a minute, wades through a litter of playthings to the livingroom, Leah with her pulltoy clicking behind like a small importunate puppy.

HEATHER
pours two inches of Tab over ice; pads out to the patio, barefoot, glass in hand, to dry her hair in the sun.

PAM
"Oh Jesus Fuck," she groans, seeing what's up, so loud Kyla rushes in to see what's the matter.

JOYCE
Ginger slouches in, weary from work; slumps at the kitchen table while Joyce stirfries.

"What kills me," Joyce lays it out to her, "is Mother still sending money when Pam asks. Here, would you cut me some of that bread Alan made this morning?"

It's being pregnant? First trimester the worst. She sprinkles Tamari on the vegetables.

PAM,
putting groceries away, worries again about her household unit, quasi-replica of the straight, pernicious, to-be-smashed Nuclear Family. Healthier, maybe, if they had other lovers?

That hypocrite, Heather, saying she hopes I'll come. Imagine if I brought Kyla, Connie with me.

JOYCE
gives herself to the pleasure of hyperbole. "Christ, she might as well be a Moonie. And for Mother to act as though I've any influence. . . The heartbreak of Pam. The endless, rotten, stinking heartbreak of Pam." *Out there in SLA country,* she thinks, but doesn't say.

There's this snapshot where she's three and Pammy's one; they're sitting in the rocker, Pammy on her lap. Pammy her big doll, almost as big as she was. *Pammy with the browngold curls, Pammy who was going to be special.*

But weren't we all three, for that matter?

HEATHER,
drowsing in late afternoon heat, decides she'll go with a long dress for the wedding. Something with lace, something demure yet striking, something modern, but a touch romantic, with a waist. For you only get married once, supposedly.

And Mother, of course, will be pleased.

JOYCE
"Well, looks like Mother misses out on her big happy family gathering," she concludes rather cruelly, adding the fried tofu. "I'm fed up with being the go-between, the good daughter, the one who holds it all together. Anyway, Alan and I just don't have the money."

PAM
"My flea bites itch me, Pam, my flea bites itch me." Kyla is in a whiny mood; LA suffers under its annual plague of fleas.

And the roaches are making a comeback in the bathroom, Pam has noticed.

Sweet bitch, said Connie in bed. Why think of that now?

JOYCE
Yes, weren't they all special, raised during the Cold War? This double message: safety, also terror. Pillar of flame, The End. Beautiful, the man said, right there in the *New York Times.* Not to her it isn't, wasn't, won't be.

Heather missed a lot of it, of course. Seven in '62 during the Missile Crisis.

Ginger: "Is something burning?" And sure enough there's an empty pot sitting on the back burner with a light under it.

PAM
ought to busy herself; sweep floor, for instance. (Idle hands are. . . the Ruling Class's workshop?) But Connie will be back any minute with the text of the new leaflet, or so she hopes. When you love, then you know. See the blaze of flame leap out of the gutter, bulletspray that knocks the woman out of her trajectory into an orbit past help. Over and over, seeing this.

*Let me say, at the risk of appearing ridiculous, that a true revolutionary is guided by great feelings of–**

But he did not mean this physical attachment.

HEATHER
"Goin' to the chapel and we're gonna get married. . . . "

Backing out of the driveway, she catches herself singing along with the radio a bit too enthusiastically. Falls silent, embarrassed. The song was way before her time, of course.

JOYCE
tries to put Leah down after dinner, but Leah, restless and irritable with humidity, won't go. Surrenders, sits with her on

---

*. . . *love.* English translation of a remark by Che Guevara, reproduced on a poster which bore his picture.

the stoop in the deepening evening, disco beat throbbing from passing radios.

Radon daughters. Who is accountable?

At least it will be a person, she tells herself, hand on belly in the ancient gesture. But is hardly persuaded.

HEATHER
takes the freeway entrance with confidence, enjoying as always the sense of control, facility with the machine. What a drag during the last gas shortage, not having this.

Gordon jokes about starting a family at the end of Western Civilization: fine thing to do to our children. To this Heather makes no reply. She wants kids too, of course, but later on; dim, amorphous beings, they wait patiently at the end of a long, long corridor, bear no obvious relation to *her* life.

PAM
makes peanutbutter on wholewheat for Kyla, joins her in front of the TV set in the tiny room knee-deep in baroque child-clutter. They watch Looney Tunes; this allays anxiety. Why? Childhood associations? Pam doesn't know, but has used the trick rather often lately. *(Let me say, at the risk of appearing ridiculous, that the true revolutionary has rarely had access to a TV set.)*

JOYCE
(while the West Coast rotates into dusk, while Alan's study group wrestles with the Black National Question) sleeps, exhausted.

HEATHER
holds the car steady at five miles over the limit, making space disappear, efficiently ticking off each familiar landmark against the list in her head. Trojan Plant cooling tower now moves into position, a mountain with a difference, cloud-capped, vomiting steam. There's some thrilling suggestion of raw power there that compels attention, has her looking back in the rear-view mirror after she's passed the spot. Protesters

back last weekend, she remembers. Gordon has pronounced them all alarmists; he ought to know, of course.

All the same, she wouldn't care to live right there in Longview.

PAM

"When's Connie coming back?" Kyla insists.

"When she gets good and ready," Pam lashes out. Fighting off panic now she tells herself a nice story, pictures the conversation on Connie's return, how, like a housewife, she'll sum up the day's events: Food Stamp office, Kyla, Heather's letter. "Going? Are you kidding? And in the middle of our organizing drive?" she'll say, as they laugh together over the engraved invitation.

HEATHER

drives. She's hungry, but not that hungry. She'll stop around Olympia for coffee.

PAM

eats peanutbutter too now, though she's not hungry. Fear, she finds, blocks thought; makes her move stiffly, with effort. As though she only wanted to huddle in a corner, conserve energy, keep a low profile, present less of a target for—?

Connie is late now, fed to the killing streets.

HEATHER

pulls into the parking lot, comes to rest beneath the sign, CAFE, mounted on stilts and visible from the interstate. It has cooled off since she started; she shivers in her tank top. Men's eyes on her half-please, half-irritate as she moves to the counter, orders a coffee, black. It's such a greasy spoon but the cream pies in their gleaming showcases look good anyway.

Of course everything looks good on 1200 calories a day.

PAM

lies on the couch in the dark, thinking of nothing. Fuzzy full moon, smog-wrapped, there behind broken blinds. Sometimes, yes, she's afraid of going crazy.

HEATHER
eases back onto I-5 in the dark, deciding maybe she loves this best of all, alone with the lights. The mysterious lights; but knowing she'll see Gordon.

PAM
At long last, the keyrattle at the door. And then Connie just stands there, hall light at her back, workshirt sleeves rolled up over muscular arms. Before she says it, Pam knows. Should have known? Did know?

"Sorry to be so late. I was over at Stella's."

Of course I don't own her. This will become Pam's mantra. Because the pain is like– Jesus. Once or twice as a kid she fell off a swing, had her breath knocked out.

HEATHER
arrives. Gordon opens the door as she comes up the driveway.

"Sweetheart, you're late. What kept you? I worried a little."

It turns him on that he takes possession next month. She ought to have shaved, she now sees, she ought to have shaved.

***

The wedding invitation arrived encased in two envelopes. Folded inside the first was the following note:

August 16

Dear Pam,

It took me a while to make up my mind to write, since it appears as though you'd rather we (the rest of the family, I mean), just left you alone. But I did want to let you know that Gordon Lindstrom and I are planning to be married. He'll be finishing his internship this month and starting a residency in a Seattle hospital. So I'll be moving up there. I think it will work out well for Mother to have me close by.

The wedding is set for September 15, a Saturday. We're just inviting the immediate family, with a larger crowd for the reception. I'm hoping Joyce will want to fly out, and I'd love to have you, of course, if you would think of coming up. I'm sure it would mean a lot to Mother if you did.

Please let me hear from you soon.

Love,
Heather

August 17

Dear Joyce,

How is summer in the big city treating you? I'm sure you're surviving, but I do hate to think of you, and Leah especially, surrounded by walls and pavement. Your Aunt Celia invited me up to Whidby Island for a week. Had a marvelous time; great weather. They've certainly done a lot of work on that cabin.

Will you be coming out for Heather's wedding? She plans to keep things very simple, but I know she'd like to have as much of the family present as possible. She seems so happy with Gordon. He's a very intelligent young man, will make a fine doctor I think, and seems to care for her a great deal too. I only wish your Father could have been with us.

I haven't heard a word as to Pam's plans. Do you think you might have any influence there? The two of you were so close as youngsters, though of course I know your views often differ now.

Gordon's family—parents, brother, and two married sisters—live in Seattle also. They're very nice people. Lutheran, but not as rigid as some I've met.

I suppose I'd better go move the sprinkler. The garden is lovely this year, roses especially. Say hello to Alan.

Love,
Mother

August 14

Dear Heather,

I was glad to get your letter. You and Gordon must care a lot for each other. Of course you know my views on the institution of marriage, so I won't go into that. I do appreciate the invitation, but won't be eligible for any more paid vacation until December, so I really don't feel I can afford to leave the city at the moment.

Excuse this short note. I'll write more another time. Right now I've got to change Leah, then go work my shift at the food co-op. I'll look forward to visiting you and Gordon next time I'm in Seattle.

Love,
Joyce

P.S. Are you changing your name to Lindstrom? What's your new address?

***

VERSIONS OF MOTHER

JOYCE

Mother in her northern suburb presides over her perfect house. Here, long ago, she played out her little drama of harassed young motherhood; but since those days the structure, like the woman, has been transformed almost past recognition by leisured, intelligent effort primed with money. Long-stemmed rose in a vase, framed prints carefully dusted, spotless crystal in the antique buffet. It is all there, yes; only the soul has fled.

Does Mother know this, sense the emptiness? Impossible to be sure, philosophy tells us; impossible to know another's pains. It may be said with certainty only that she moves deliberately through the rooms, refusing to admit the necessity for haste, the possibility of panic. All decisions made (but when? how?), there is only, now, a choreographed precision.

PAM

Mother sits drinking her Colombian coffee, reading the *Wall Street Journal*; phones her broker and, long distance, Peruvian Indians groan under the lash; the screw tightens on factory hands in Manila. Mother in her neat four-bedroom mansion with the electric heat, dishwasher, Cuisinart, knife sharpener, disposal unit, hedge clipper, consumes in a year enough energy to maintain an entire village in India.

HEATHER
Mother's been helpful with the wedding details. She likes having something like that to get involved in. She doesn't have much of a life, after all, with Father gone. Still, no reason why she couldn't marry again, if she really wanted. She's an attractive woman. She'd look fantastic if she'd lose ten pounds. They say the market is glutted with widows her age, but she could try at least. Go out sometimes, make an effort. As it is, she makes you feel so responsible.

And then it's no picnic being the one normal daughter.

***

MOTHER'S SCOTCH
OR
PAMMY AND JOCELYN

Pam and Joyce attend the wedding after all, as it happens, converging on Sea-Tac airport aboard flights conveniently fifteen minutes apart. Mother collects them, scoops them into the car as she did in the old days after the ballet lessons. Totes them home along the familiar strip of freeway past the newly sharpened, sinister urban skyline. Later, they meet in the former "Pammy's room," though the up-to-date fabrics, the lamps in sophisticated shapes, now hold no hint of anything Pam remembers.

"Alone at last," Joyce murmurs, a certain defensive irony in her voice. She has whacked her hair off again, but looks, for all that, fairly respectable in a floor-length Indian-print skirt.

"Where's Heather?" Pam sits cross-legged on the bed, wearing tennis shoes, smoking Bull Durham.

"Washing her chestnut locks. Big Game tomorrow, you know."

"Hot dog." Pam makes the face that in childhood signified *ick*. "Well, shall we drink to survival?"

Joyce frowns at the proffered bottle. "Mother's Scotch?"

"Myself, I never buy anything but Chivas Regal."

"Dammit, Pam, you know she wouldn't like it."

"She offered us drinks at dinner. I declined. Though it might have made Gordon an easier pill to swallow. Who's to know? She took a Seconal at ten o'clock."

"Don't tell me she doesn't know what's in there."

"We could water it."

" 'Long Day's Journey into Night,' perhaps?"

"I fail to catch the allusion."

"Okay, okay, pour."

When they were little, Pam "egged" Joyce on, Mother said. Pam the brilliant concocter of mischief, Joyce the good, was how it mostly broke down. It was only after registering virtuous objection that Joyce sometimes succumbed to the sin at hand. Later, during adolescence, she led, briefly, in daring: going all the way with boys, hash, dexedrine. . . "Hardly the proper thing for the first trimester," she comments now, accepting the poisoned cup, a blue plastic number commandeered from its place in the bathroom next to the toothbrushes.

Pam sits there up against the wall clutching the bottle, looking romantically disreputable in sweatshirt, army pants. Mother Teresa in urban guerrilla getup.

Does Pam know she is thus regarded? Perhaps. At any rate, both she and Joyce remember vividly their disastrous last encounter; on the third day of her visit to LA, as Pam continued her rundown of political tendencies in that beleaguered city, Joyce had lost control and blurted, "Don't talk to me about your religion." Now they opt for safety: Gordon; the Personal.

"Typical pig MD," Pam assesses flatly. "I could practically see him clutching his balls under the dinner table when I made that nasty comment about the Pill. He hates to have his sacred authority questioned."

"I wonder how Heather explains the two of us."

"Oh *you're* not so bad. Plenty of unwed mothers in the world these days."

"Thanks, buddy."

"No offense intended. You're pregnant again, I take it?"

"Looks that way."

"Congratulations. I mean, assuming congratulations are in order."

"Well, actually—"

"Don't tell me you don't want it."

Joyce hesitates. Firstborn, programmed to win, to know what she wants, she finds this difficult. "Shit, Pam, I don't know. We always planned on another."

"Is that any reason?"

"No, of course it isn't. It's just that I don't understand why I should be feeling what I'm feeling. I'm so depressed all the time; I keep thinking maybe it's hormones. And Alan's ecstatic, of course."

"Nevertheless, it's your body."

"I'm painfully aware of that fact. I just. . . I can't think about it right now. That's why I came, I suppose. To get some distance, if such a thing exists."

"Probably not."

"No, probably not. What about you?"

"What *about* me? Pam is absorbed in the manual intricacies of rolling herself another cigarette.

"How are you doing, I mean?"

"Oh, I'm okay." Her curved pink tongue emerges, takes a long time to slide the length of the rolling paper.

"Care to be a bit more specific?"

Pam has always been difficult like this; now she lights the cigarette, takes a leisurely swig of Scotch straight from the bottle, wipes her mouth with the back of her hand.

"Pam?"

"Well, things could be worse, I guess. They could sure be better. Connie's going at it hot and heavy with this woman

Stella, who I can't stand. Kyla's mother's been writing from Salt Lake City, threatening to come get her, though I doubt she'll do it.

"Lovely. Who is this Stella?"

"Oh, she's a fine person, Party member and all. Non-monogamy isn't the issue of course; Connie and I have always agreed about that. But Stella and I have never liked each other, so for Connie to get involved with her. . . and then, as it happens, the Party's started a major organizing drive, which means we all have to see a lot of each other. It wasn't so cool that I left, really, in the middle of everything, but Mother called up and put the heat on, and I—"

You know which side your bread's buttered on, Joyce wants to finish snidely, though she doesn't. It's not true, she knows; Pam doesn't get all that much money from Mother, and would be quite prepared to do without it rather than compromise a single one of her sacred political principles. The words that come out are as dangerous, though kinder: "Pammy, I wish you'd quit."

"Quit what?" Pam isn't having any, thank you.

"You know."

"I do?"

"The NCP."

"Jocelyn."

Joyce's "real" name; Pam had loved using it when they were little. It said: older sister. It said: prissy snot. She flings it down now in lieu of the damning phrase she will later use, summing up Joyce for Connie's benefit: *my sister, the liberal.*

Joyce forges wearily on. "All right, so you don't want to hear it. But Pam, I worry about you. I just don't want to see you get hurt."

"You don't want to see *me* get hurt. Forget Watts, forget El Barrio—"

"You know that's not what I mean. It's. . . sectarian groups make people crazy, Pam. It's isolating. You end up talking to yourself."

"Preach, sister. You sound like the *Guardian*."

"Maybe I do."

"Look, make up your mind. Do you want to talk politics? Because last time, as I recall, you said you didn't."

"It's not even about politics. It's about what works and what doesn't."

"Now you're beginning to sound a lot like Mother."

This, surely, is the verbal equivalent of the slap Pam would once have delivered, aggravated past endurance by her consciousness of Joyce's unfair advantage, the power eighteen extra months on earth would eternally vest in her. And Joyce would have flung howling from the room, screaming for Mother.

"All right, have it your way," she answers, grownup now; sits there fuming at Pam's ingratitude.

But the charged moment passes. They speak of other things: Leah, Kyla, Los Angeles versus New York. They drink to dull perception. They diagnose.

"Mother seems pretty cheerful, don't you think?"

"Cheerful?" Pam snorts, "Why wouldn't she be cheerful?" (this, too, being an old dispute between them, though less explosive than the other).

"She would, being Mother. I don't know how she does it."

"Are you kidding, an upper-middle-class woman, privileged as hell? You bet she's cheerful."

But Joyce, touched by Scotch, hardly listens. "Who is Mother, anyway?" she wants to know.

"What's that supposed to mean?"

"Like, what's she really about, what does she want? What did she think she was doing, having us? Why does she bother to get up in the morning?"

"I don't see what you're getting at. She lives exactly the same way most of her neighbors do."

"Everything in this place is so perfect, elegant. But surface only. Hollow. Robbed of context."

"So?" It is not precisely a hostile question. Pam retains her critical faculties; Joyce, stoned, seems overly credulous, as though none of this had ever occurred to her before.

"So. . . this is what made us."

"You know I don't buy that psychoanalytic crap."

Joyce just smiles. "You know what I think of when I'm in this house? There's this poem by Baudelaire," and she recites:

> Mon enfant, ma soeur,
> Songe à la douceur
> D'aller là-bas vivre ensemble!. . .
>
> La, tout n'est qu'ordre et beauté,
> Luxe, calme et volupté.*

"I don't know about the *volupté* part," Pam comments drily, forgetting to pretend she never took French.

But Joyce is prostrate, sobbing on the bed, having glimpsed, in a flash, the terrible fate of the family. She's drunk, she knows, but it seems so horribly sad. And now she's started crying she can't stop, buries her face in the pillow. Mother's designer pillowcase all fouled with tears and snot.

"This is silly," she want to admit, but is crying too hard. She dislikes dreadfully breaking down in front of Pam. It reminds her somehow of the time they took acid together: Pam's first trip, and Joyce was going to guide her. Well, it's obvious how that one turned out: Pam ecstatic, like a kid with a new toy; Joyce miserable, paranoid, bumming.

And then, rather astonished, she hears herself moan, "I'm so angry, Pam, I'm just so bloody angry."

"At whom?" Pam inquires, rational to the last.

"I don't know."

Pam, frightened, touches her finally, when she has to.

Heather has her wedding, for what it's worth.

***

HEATHER

Ladies and gentlemen, at this time we'd like to take a few moments to call your attention to some of the safety features of this McDonnell Douglas DC-10.

---

* My child, my sister,/think of the sweetness/of going there to live together. . . /There, there is nothing but order and beauty,/luxury, calm and voluptuousness.

"Thank god that's over with," Heather sighs, luxuriating in a sense of earned weariness. "I guess you just shouldn't expect to enjoy your own wedding."

"Oh, I didn't think it was that bad." Gordon is holding her left hand, running his forefinger over the unfamiliar ridge the ring makes.

In the unlikely event that our altitude should change suddenly, causing a change in cabin pressure, an oxygen mask will appear above your seat. Extinguish all smoking materials, pull the mask firmly toward you to start the flow of oxygen, place the mask over your face, and continue to breathe freely.

"Well, not for you, of course. You didn't have all those details to worry about."

"I guess you're right, honey. I'm sorry, I didn't realize—"

"Never mind," she reassures him. "It's over now."

"You looked fantastic, if it's any consolation."

Ladies and gentlemen, at this time we'd like to ask you to extinguish all smoking materials, make sure that your seatbelts are securely fastened, and your seatbacks and traytables are in their full upright position.

"And then Joyce and Pam," she frets.

"Oh, I thought Joyce was okay. Pam was a little weird, maybe," but their brother-in-law chuckles indulgently.

"Wearing that leather vest to the reception! What a crew! Now we're safely married I guess I can ask, do you suppose it's genetic?"

They laugh together, very much pleased with themselves. "Well, you did invite them," Gordon points out reasonably.

"What was I going to do? They *are* my sisters."

Flight attendants, prepare for departure.

JOYCE

Flight attendants, prepare for departure.

Strapped into her window seat just back of the right wing watching Puget Sound drop away beneath her, Joyce approaches her existential situation with heroic detachment. *If we should fail, fall screaming out of this sky, I anyway wouldn't have to have the kid.*

PAM

"Excuse me, young woman, could you tell me the name of that mountain?" She's the little old lady from Pasadena or someplace, flesh cascading down her neck in soft pink turkey-wattles, spectacles thick before rheumy faded blue eyes.

"Rainier," Pam snarls, wishing she could remember what the Indians called it. It's the ghost of a mountain, really, glimpsed through smog.

Flight attendants, prepare for departure.

God, airplanes are ugly. White faces surround her. Bad trip.

JOYCE, PAM, HEATHER

Three airplanes rip the belly of the sky. Three sisters are blasted into the upper air.

PAM

Later, she stands in front of the Food Stamp office, dispensing leaflets with a practiced gesture. "Come on, read about it, read all about the organizing drive to combat police brutality, read about how you can put a stop to police terror in your community. . . . "

It is another warm smoggy day; fall-like, perhaps, as LA understands fall. To the east and south the hills burn. Down the block stands Connie, and across the street in the choice spot, vaguely shaded by a mangy palm tree, is Stella, reeling off an identical rap. *Just one big happy commie family.*

Existence is suffering, so the Buddhists claim. But they are idealists, not materialists, and thus can afford to claim this.

Whatever she's got to handle, she'll handle, Pam figures.

JOYCE

lies there quietly, good girl, on the clean table of the modern, safe, legal abortionist, awaiting anaesthetic. She feels, will feel, nothing; so she has been promised. Not even the anger.

HEATHER

reclines on the redwood deck of Gordon's parents' place at Tahoe, sipping a Tab (having gained back three of the five pounds lost before the wedding). Below, the lake glints, precious and cold as diamonds. It's late September, chilly in the sun.

Beside her on the table is her tasteful notepaper, her list of wedding gifts. *Dr. and Mrs. Gordon Lindstrom, 6483 E. Franklin Terrace, Seattle, Wash.,* she is carefully inscribing in the corner of each envelope. She plans a sort of assembly line procedure for her thankyou notes, looks forward to being able to announce an efficient completion.

She has arrived, yes. In a minute Gordon will open the sliding glass door and say, "How about some lunch?"

JOYCE,
her wound. Her question in the dark: *Who is Mother, creator of all this?*